Happy
PEOPLE
READ &
Drink
COFFEE

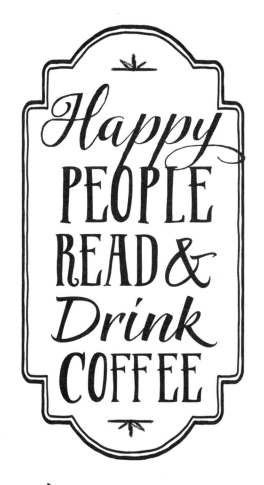

Happy PEOPLE READ & Drink COFFEE

AGNÈS MARTIN-LUGAND

ALLEN&UNWIN

First published in Great Britain in 2016 by Allen & Unwin
This paperback edition published in Great Britain in 2017 by Allen & Unwin

First published in the United States by Weinstein Books, a member of the
Perseus Books Group

Originally published in France by Éditions Michel Lafon in 2013 under the
title *Les gens heureux lisent et boivent du café*

Copyright © Éditions Michel Lafon, 2013

Translation copyright © Sandra Smith, 2014

Allen & Unwin
c/o Atlantic Books
Ormond House
26–27 Boswell Street
London WC1N 3JZ
Phone: 020 7269 1610
Fax: 020 7430 0916
Email: UK@allenandunwin.com
Web: www.allenandunwin.com/uk

A CIP catalogue record for this book is available from the British Library.

Paperback ISBN 978 1 76029 171 6
E-Book ISBN 978 1 92526 865 2

Set in 11/17 pt Sabon LT Std by Post Pre-press Group, Australia
Printed in Great Britain by Clays Ltd, St Ives plc

10 9 8 7 6 5 4 3 2 1

1

"Mom, *please?*"

"I said no, Clara."

"Oh, come on, Diane. Let her go with me."

"Don't think you can fool me, Colin. If Clara goes with you, the two of you will take absolutely no notice of the time and we'll end up leaving for vacation three days late."

"Come with us then. That way, you can keep an eye on us!"

"Absolutely not. Have you seen how much I still have to do?"

"Even more reason for Clara to come with me, you'll have lots of peace and quiet."

"Mom!"

"Fine. Off you go! Scoot! Disappear, the both of you."

They left, laughing and fooling around as they went downstairs.

I found out they were still fooling around in the car when the truck crashed into them. I told myself they were still laughing when they died. I told myself that I should have been with them.

And for the past year, I've told myself I should have died with them. I tell myself that every day. But my heart stubbornly keeps on beating. And I'm still alive. Utterly miserable and still alive.

Sprawled out on the sofa, I was watching my cigarette smoke rise into the air when the front door opened. Felix no longer waited for me to invite him to come over. He simply appeared with no warning, or almost. Ever since we met at college, I'd learned how to deal with his faults. My oldest friend, and my business partner, he came over every day. Why on earth did I give him that spare set of keys?

I started when he came in, and ashes fell on my pajamas. I blew them off onto the floor. I went into the kitchen to get my next fix of caffeine so I wouldn't see him start to clean up, which he did every day.

When I got back, nothing had been moved. The ashtrays were still overflowing; empty cups, takeout containers, and bottles were strewn all over the coffee table. Felix had sat down, cross-legged, and was staring at me. Seeing him looking so serious upset me for a split second, but what surprised me more was what he was wearing. Why was he in a suit? What had happened to his torn jeans and tight-fitting T-shirt, the only clothes he ever wore?

"Where are you going dressed like that? A wedding or a funeral?"

"What time is it?" He was eyeing me carefully.

"You haven't answered my question. I don't give a damn what time it is. Did you dress up like that to pick up some stock market type?"

"I wish. It's two o'clock and you have to go get washed and dressed. You can't go looking like that."

"Where do you think I'm going?"

"Hurry up. Your parents and Colin's will be waiting for us. We have to be there in an hour."

My entire body started to shake, my hands began to tremble; I felt sick.

"Out of the question. I won't go to the cemetery. You hear me?"

"Do it for them," he said softly. "Come and pay your respects; today's the day, you have to go, it's been a year, everyone will be there to support you."

"I don't want anyone's support. I refuse to go to this stupid memorial service. Do you really think I want to celebrate their deaths?"

My voice was trembling and the first tears of the day began to fall. Through the mist, I could see Felix standing up and walking towards me. He wrapped his arms around me and crushed me to his chest.

"Diane, please, come for them."

I angrily pushed him away.

"I said no; are you that stupid?" I shouted when I saw him about to take a step closer. "Get out of my house!"

I ran into my bedroom. In spite of my trembling hands, I managed to lock myself inside. I collapsed against the door, hugging my legs to my chest. The silence that filled the apartment was broken by Felix's sigh.

"I'll come back tonight."

"I never want to see you again."

"At least make the effort to get washed, otherwise I'll throw you into the shower myself."

His footsteps faded away, and when I heard the door slam, I knew he'd finally gone.

For a long time, I sat there, drained, my head resting on my knees, before glancing over to my bed. With great difficulty, I crawled towards it on all fours. I hoisted myself up and wrapped my duvet around me. As soon as I was in my safe place, I started searching for a hint of Colin's odor. The smell of him had disappeared long ago, even though I had never changed the sheets. I wanted to smell him again. I wanted to forget the stench of the hospital, the stench of death that had soaked into his skin the last time I rested my head against his neck.

I wanted to sleep, sleep would help me forget.

One year before, when I arrived at the Emergency Room with Felix, they told me it was too late, they told me that my daughter had died in the ambulance. The doctors gave me just enough time to throw up before telling me it was only a matter of minutes, possibly hours, for Colin. If I wanted to say goodbye, I had no time to lose. I wanted to scream, to shout that they were lying, but I couldn't. I had fallen headlong into a nightmare; I wanted to believe I would soon wake up. A nurse led us to Colin's bedside.

From the moment I entered that room, every word, every gesture became engraved in my memory. Colin was stretched out in the bed, hooked up to innumerable machines, noisy, flashing machines. He could barely move; his face was covered in bruises. I stood there for several minutes, totally incapable of moving because of what I was seeing. Felix had come with me, and his presence prevented me from breaking down completely. Colin turned his head slightly to look at me, his eyes fixed on mine. He found the strength to try to smile. That smile made it possible for me to go over to him. I took his hand; he squeezed mine.

"You should be with Clara," he said, even though it was hard for him to talk.

"Colin, Clara is—"

"She's in the operating room," Felix, said, quickly cutting me off.

I looked up at him. He was smiling at Colin and wouldn't look at me. My ears were ringing; my whole body was shaking; I could barely see. I felt Colin squeeze my hand tighter. I watched him as he listened to Felix give him news of Clara, explaining she was going to pull through. That lie cruelly brought me back to reality. In a broken voice, Colin told me he hadn't seen the truck; he'd been singing with Clara. I had lost the ability to speak. I leaned towards him, stroking his hair and forehead. He turned his face to look at me again. My tears made his features look blurred; he had already begun to disappear; I couldn't breathe. He raised his hand to hold it against my cheek.

"Hush now, my love," he said. "Calm down; you heard Felix. Clara's going to need you."

There was no way I could escape the look in his eyes, so full of hope for our daughter.

"But what about you?" I managed to say.

"She's the one who counts," he said, wiping a tear from my cheek.

I was sobbing even harder, resting my face against the palm of his hand. It was still warm. He was still here. Still. I clung to that idea: still here.

"Colin," I whispered. "I can't lose you."

"You're not alone, you have Clara, and Felix will take good care of the two of you."

I shook my head, not daring to look at him.

"Everything's going to be all right, my love, you have to be brave, for our daughter . . ."

His voice suddenly went very quiet; I panicked and looked up at him. He seemed so tired. He had used his last bit of strength for me, as always. I pressed myself against him to kiss him; he responded with the last bit of life within him. I stretched out alongside him and helped him lay his head on my shoulder. As long as he was in my arms, he couldn't leave me. Colin whispered that he loved me, one last time; I barely had time to say I loved him, too, when he peacefully passed away. For several hours, I held him, I rocked him in my arms, kissed him, breathed him in. When my parents tried to get me to leave, I screamed. Colin's parents had come to see their son, but I wouldn't let them touch him. He was mine and mine alone. It was Felix's patience that finally forced me to give in. He had taken his time to calm me down before reminding me that I also had to say goodbye to Clara. My daughter had always been the only person in the world who could tear me away from Colin. Death had changed nothing. I released my grip on his body. I kissed him on the lips one last time and left.

I was lost in a fog as I walked towards Clara. I only reacted when I was in front of the door to the private room where they'd put her.

"No," I said to Felix. "I can't."

"Diane, you should go and see her."

Staring at the door, I took a few steps back before turning and rushing down the corridors of the hospital. I refused to see my daughter dead. I only wanted to remember her smile, her messy blond curls flying around her face, her mischievous, sparkling eyes on the very morning she had left with her father.

Today, as every day for the past year, utter silence reigned in our apartment. No music, no laughter, no endless conversations.

My legs automatically took me to Clara's bedroom. Everything in it was pink. From the moment I'd known we were having a girl, I'd insisted that the entire room be decorated in that color. Colin had used a phenomenal number of sly tricks to get me to change my mind. But I never gave in.

I had touched nothing; not her duvet, still rolled up in a ball, not her toys scattered all over the room, not her nightgown left on the floor, not her little suitcase with wheels where she'd put her dolls to go away on vacation. Only two things were no longer in her room: the fluffy security blanket she'd taken with her and the one I slept with.

After silently closing the door, I made my way to Colin's dressing room where I picked up a new shirt.

I had just locked myself in the bathroom to take a shower when I heard Felix come in. In the bathroom, a large sheet covered the mirror and all the shelves were empty except for Colin's cologne. No beauty products, no makeup, no creams, no jewelry.

The cold bathroom tiles had no effect on me; I couldn't care less. Water flowed over my body without making me feel any better at all. I filled my hand with Clara's strawberry shampoo. Its sweet smell brought tears to my eyes along with a morbid sense of comfort.

My ritual could begin. I sprayed myself with Colin's cologne, the first layer of protection. I closed the buttons of his shirt, second layer. I pulled on his hooded sweatshirt, third layer. I tied up my damp hair to keep the smell of strawberries longer, fourth layer.

In the living room, my garbage had all disappeared, the windows were open and it sounded like there was a battle going on in the kitchen. Before joining Felix, I closed the shutters in the living room. The semi-darkness was my best friend.

Felix had his head in the freezer. I leaned against the doorframe and watched him. He'd put his normal uniform back on and was shaking his bottom and whistling.

"May I ask what's put you in such a good mood?"

"The night I had yesterday. Let me make dinner and I'll tell you everything."

He had turned towards me and was staring. He came over to me and took several deep breaths.

"Stop sniffing me like a dog," I said.

"You've got to stop that."

"What are you complaining about? I got washed."

"It's about time."

He gave me a peck on the cheek before getting back to work.

"Since when do you know how to cook?"

"I don't cook; I use a microwave. And I still need to find something good enough to eat. Your fridge is worse than the Gobi Desert."

"If you're hungry, order a pizza. You can't cook anything. You'd even mess up a frozen dinner."

"And that's why you and Colin kept me fed, these past ten years. You've just had a brilliant idea; I'll have more time to spend with you."

I went and collapsed on the sofa. I was going to have the privilege of hearing all about his fantastic night. A glass of red wine quickly appeared in front of me. Felix sat down opposite me and threw over his pack of cigarettes. I lit one right away.

"Your parents send their love."

"Good for them," I replied, blowing smoke towards him.

"They're worried about you," he said, sighing.

"They shouldn't be."

"They'd like to come and see you."

"Well, I don't want to see them. You're the only one I can tolerate seeing, lucky you."

"I'm irreplaceable; you just can't do without me."

"Felix!"

"Fine, if you insist, I'll give you all the juicy details about what I did last night."

"Oh, no! Anything but your sex life!"

"Make up your mind. It's either my sexual exploits or your parents."

"OK. Go ahead, I'm listening."

Felix spared me none of the gory details. To him, life was just one gigantic party, spiced up by unbridled sexuality and by being the first to try illegal substances. Once he was in full flight, he didn't even wait for me to reply, he just kept talking, nonstop. He didn't even pause for breath when the doorbell rang.

The delivery guy also heard how Felix got himself invited to share the bed of a twenty-year-old student. Another one Felix decided to teach a thing or two.

"If you could have seen the expression on his face this morning, poor little sweetie; I was sure he was about to beg me to come back and take care of him. I was so moved," he added, pretending to wipe away a tear.

"You are really disgusting!"

"I did warn him, but what can I do? Once you've had a taste of Felix, you get addicted."

While I had only toyed with two or three bites, he was clearly full enough to burst. He still didn't look like he was going to leave. He had become strangely silent; he took the leftovers and disappeared into the kitchen.

"Diane. You haven't even asked me how it went today."

"I'm not interested."

"You're going too far. How can you be so indifferent?"

"Shut up, I'm anything but indifferent. How dare you say something like that to me!" I shouted, quickly jumping to my feet.

"Shit, look at you; you look like a total wreck. You don't do anything any more. You don't work.

Your whole life consists of smoking, drinking, and sleeping. Your apartment has turned into a sanctuary. I can't stand watching you sink deeper and deeper into a hole every day."

"No one can understand."

"Of course they can, everyone understands what you're going through. But that's no reason to die little by little. It's been a year since they're gone, it's time to start living again. Fight. Do it for Colin and Clara."

"I don't know how to fight, and anyway, I don't want to."

"Let me help you."

I couldn't stand it any more, so I put my hands over my ears and closed my eyes. Felix took me in his arms and forced me to sit down. He still wanted to give me one of his suffocating hugs. I never understood why he needed to crush me against him.

"Why don't you go out with me tonight?" he asked.

"You haven't understood a thing I've said," I replied, snuggling against him in spite of myself.

"Go outside, be with people. You can't remain a recluse any more. Come to Happy People with me tomorrow. The bookstore needs you, and you need to get out."

"I couldn't care less about Happy People!"

"Well, if that's true, then let's go away on vacation together. I can close the bookstore. They can do without us in the neighborhood . . . well, they can certainly do without me for a few weeks."

"I don't feel like going on vacation."

"I'm sure you do. We'll have a really fun time, just the two of us, and I'll be able to take care of you every minute of the day. It's what you need to get you back on track."

He couldn't see my eyes popping out of my head at the idea of having him permanently on my back.

"Listen, let me think about it," I said, to appease him.

"Promise?"

"Yes. I want to go to sleep now, so get going."

He gave me a noisy kiss on the cheek before taking his cell phone out of his pocket. He flipped through his impressively large address book before calling one of his Stevens, Freds, or yet another Alex. Fired up by the idea of the evening of debauchery that awaited him, he finally let go of me. I stood up and lit a cigarette before heading for the front door. He stopped talking to the person on the other end of the phone long enough to kiss me one last time.

"I'll come tomorrow," he whispered in my ear, "but don't count on seeing me too early; I'm going to have a very busy night tonight."

My only reply was to raise my eyes to heaven. Happy People wouldn't open on time again tomorrow morning. There really wasn't much I could do about it. It was in another life that I had run a literary café. Felix had worn me out. Lord knows I love him, but I'd had enough.

Once in bed, I went over his words in my head. He seemed determined to get me to do something. I had to find a way out of it at all costs. Whenever he had an idea like that, nothing could stop him. He wanted me to get better, but I didn't. What excuse could I make up?

2

A week had passed since Felix had launched his plan to "Pull Diane out of her depression". He'd kept bombarding me with suggestions, each one more far-fetched than the last. I reached a breaking point when he left some vacation brochures on the coffee table. I knew full well what he had in mind: fun in the sun with everything that entailed. A kind of Club Med, lounge chairs, palm trees, watered-down rum cocktails, glistening, tanned bodies, water aerobic classes where you could ogle the activities organizer—a dream for Felix and a nightmare for me. All those holidaymakers crushed against each other on a tiny beach, or fighting to get to the buffet in their fancy evening clothes, appalled at the idea that their snoring neighbor might steal the last sausage, all those people happy to have been locked up in a tiny plane with screaming children around them: everything about it made me want to puke.

That's why I was walking around in circles, smoking so much that my throat was on fire. Sleep was no longer a refuge for me; it had been invaded by visions of Felix in a bathing suit forcing me to go salsa dancing in a nightclub. He wouldn't let the idea go as long as I refused to give in. I had to find a way to get out of it, nip it in the bud, reassure him while getting him off my back. Staying at home was out. Going away, leaving Paris for good was the only solution in the end. Finding some isolated spot where he wouldn't follow me.

A trip into the world of the living was becoming inevitable: my kitchen cabinets and fridge were hopelessly empty. All I could find were out-of-date packages of cookies—Clara's snacks—and some of Colin's beer. I took one of the bottles and turned it round and round before deciding to open it. I breathed it in as if it had the bouquet of an extremely expensive wine. I took a sip and memories flooded through me.

Our first kiss had the taste of beer. How many times had we laughed about that? Romanticism wasn't our strong suit when we were twenty. Colin only drank brown ale; he didn't like lager. He always said he wondered why he had chosen a blond like me, which invariably resulted in him getting a slap on the back of the head.

Beer had also once interfered with our choice of where to go on vacation. Colin had wanted to go to Ireland for a few days. Then he'd pretended that the rain, wind, and cold made him change his mind. In truth, he knew I only liked going to sunny places where I could get a tan, so he didn't want to force me to wear a windbreaker and fleece jacket on our summer vacation, or make me go somewhere I wouldn't have enjoyed.

I dropped the bottle and it shattered on the tiled floor.

Sitting at Colin's desk with an atlas in front of me, I looked over the map of Ireland. How could I choose my tomb under an open sky? How could I find a place that would bring me the peace and tranquility I needed to be alone with Colin and Clara? Knowing absolutely nothing about Ireland, and finding myself unable to choose somewhere to settle, I ended up closing my eyes and letting my fingers land on the map, trusting to fate.

I half-opened one eye and looked closer. I opened the other eye after taking my finger away, to see the name of the place. Fate had chosen the tiniest village possible; I could barely make out its name on the map. Mulranny. I would go into exile in Mulranny.

The moment had come: I had to tell Felix that I was going away, to live in Ireland. Three days— it took three whole days to build up the courage to do it. We'd just finished dinner; I'd forced myself to eat every mouthful to please him. Slumped down in an armchair, he was leafing through one of his brochures.

"Felix, put down the magazines."

"You've made up your mind?"

He jumped up and rubbed his hands together.

"Where are we going?"

"I have no idea where you're going but I'm going to live in Ireland."

I was trying to sound as normal as possible. Felix was gasping for air like a fish out of water.

"Calm down."

"Are you kidding? You can't be serious! Who could have put such an idea in your head?"

"Colin. Go figure."

"That's it. She's finally gone mad. Are you telling me that he came back from the dead to tell you where you should go?"

"You don't have to be mean. He would have liked to go there, that's all. I'll go in his place."

"Oh no you won't," said Felix, sounding very sure of himself.

"And why not?"

"What on earth will you do in that land of . . . of . . ."

"Of what?"

"Of rugby players and mutton eaters."

"Rugby players annoy you? First I've heard of it. Normally they seem to attract you. And do you think it would be better to go to Thailand to get high on some beach during the full moon and come back with 'Brandon forever' tattooed on my ass?"

"Touché . . . bitch. But it's not the same. You're already in a bad state; you'll end up beyond redemption."

"Stop. I've decided to go to Ireland for a few months; you've got nothing to say about it."

"Don't think I'm going to go with you."

I stood up and started straightening up anything I happened to find.

"So much the better, because you're not invited. I've had enough of having you follow me around like a little puppy. You're suffocating me!" I cried, looking at him.

"Well, you just think about this: I'll soon be suffocating you again."

He burst out laughing and without taking his eyes off of me, lit a cigarette.

"You want to know why? Because I give you no more than two days. You'll come back all apologetic and beg me to take you somewhere sunny."

"Not on my life. Think what you want, but I'm going there to try to get better."

"You're going about it the wrong way, but at least you seem more cheerful."

"Don't you have friends waiting for you somewhere?"

I couldn't stand his prying looks any more. He stood up and came over to me.

"You want me to go to celebrate your new idiotic idea?"

His face clouded over. He put his hands on my shoulders and looked straight into my eyes.

"Are you really trying to get better?"

"Of course."

"So you agree that you won't pack any of Colin's shirts, none of Clara's stuffed animals, no perfume except your own."

I'd been caught in my own trap. My stomach hurt, my head hurt, everything hurt. Impossible to escape his dark eyes, as dark as coal, or his fingers digging into my shoulders.

"Of course I want to get better; I'm going to

distance myself from their things little by little. You should be happy; you've been wanting me to do it for such a long time."

By some miracle, my voice had not given me away. Felix sighed deeply.

"You're irresponsible. You'll never manage it. Colin would have never let you do such a thing. It's good that you want to find a way to get better, but please, forget this idea; we'll find some other way. I'm afraid you'll bury yourself even more."

"I'm not going to forget it."

"Go and get some sleep. We'll talk about it again tomorrow."

He made a sad face, kissed me on the cheek and walked towards the door without saying another word.

Once in bed, curled up in my duvet with Clara's cuddly toy held tightly in my arms, I tried to calm my racing heart. Felix was wrong; Colin would have let me go abroad alone, on condition that he'd planned everything. He took care of all the details whenever we went away, from the airplane tickets to the hotel reservations to the passports. He never would have let me be in charge of my passport or Clara's; he said I was too disorganized. So would he have trusted me to take on such a project? I couldn't say for sure, in truth.

I'd never lived alone; I'd left my parents' house to move in with him. I was afraid to make a simple telephone call to ask for information or make a complaint. Colin was the one who knew how to do everything. I had to imagine he was guiding me to get everything ready. I was going to make him proud of me. If it was the last thing I did before burying myself alive, I would prove to everyone that I was capable of seeing this through.

Certain things didn't change, like the way I packed my bags. My closet was empty and my suitcases ready to burst. I would only use a fraction of the things I'd packed. All that was missing was some reading material, and I had to be strict with myself.

How long had it been since I'd been to the bookstore? Felix was going to collapse behind the counter when he saw me. In less than five minutes

I'd reached the Rue Vieille-du-Temple. My street. Long ago, I'd spent my days here; in the sidewalk cafés, in the boutiques, in the galleries and at work. Just being here made me happy, before.

Today, hidden under the hood of one of Colin's sweatshirts, I fled from the store windows, the people who lived there, the tourists. I walked on the road to avoid all the damned posts that make you weave in and out. Everything felt stressful, even the delicious smell of warm bread coming from the bakery where I used to shop.

I slowed down as I got closer to Happy People. More than a year had passed since I'd set foot inside. I stopped on the sidewalk opposite without even glancing up at it. Standing dead still, I dug into one of my pockets; I needed a cigarette. Someone bumped into me and I inadvertently turned my face towards my literary café. Its little wooden window, the door in the middle with the bell inside, the name I'd chosen five years before with the sign, Happy People Read and Drink Coffee, everything took me back to my former life with Colin and Clara.

Once I'd gotten my degree, my parents were in

total despair about my inactivity, so they'd pulled out their checkbook. I made the mistake of saying that I'd like to work in a bookstore that was also a café. Colin was already a partner at his law firm and was enthusiastic about the idea. They'd agreed on starting the business: my parents had approved and they bought the literary café. Ever since Colin and Clara had died, my parents regularly pumped money into the place. As for me, I lived off of Colin's life insurance and the compensation I'd collected. The morning of the opening stuck in my mind as one of general panic. The construction work wasn't finished and we hadn't unpacked all the books. Felix hadn't arrived yet; I had to fight with the workmen alone so they'd get a move on. Colin called me every fifteen minutes to make sure we'd be ready for the opening that night. Each time, I'd held back my tears and laughed like an idiot. My very dear partner, looking as smart as anything, deigned to show up in the middle of the afternoon, while I was on the verge of a nervous breakdown because the sign still wasn't hung above the door.

"Felix, where have you been?" I shouted.

"At the hairdresser's. And you should have done the same," he replied, grabbing a lock of my hair with a disdainful look on his face.

"And just when was I supposed to do that? Nothing is ready for tonight, I've been lying to Colin since this morning. I knew all along this was destined for disaster; this place is more a curse than a blessing. Why did my parents and Colin listen to me when I told them I wanted to open a literary café? I want nothing more to do with it."

My voice reached screaming pitch and I started rushing around in all directions, trying to do everything. Felix told all the workmen to get out and came over to me. He grabbed me and shook me hard.

"Enough! From now on, I'm in charge. Go and get ready."

"There's not enough time!"

"It is out of the question that we open with an owner who looks like a Gorgon."

He pushed me out of the back door, the one that led to the studio that came with the café. Inside, I found a new dress and everything I needed to look pretty. An enormous bouquet of roses and freesias lay on the floor. I read Colin's note. He told me again how much he believed in me.

Opening night was a great success in the end, in spite of our accounts that showed virtually no profit—Felix declared himself responsible for the cash register. Colin's winks and smiles encouraged me. I walked from table to table with Clara in my arms, between family, friends, my husband's colleagues, Felix's dubious acquaintances, and other shopkeepers from the street.

Today, five years later, everything had changed. Colin and Clara were gone. I had no desire whatsoever to go back to work and everything in this place reminded me of my husband and my child. How proud Colin had been when he'd come to celebrate there—winning in court, Clara taking her first steps among the clients, the first time she wrote her name while sitting at the counter with a glass of grenadine.

A shadow appeared on the sidewalk beside me. Felix clutched me close to him and rocked me in his arms.

"You know you've been standing here for half an hour; come with me."

I shook my head.

"You didn't come for no reason; it's time you came back to Happy People."

He held my hand and walked me across the street. He squeezed it when he pushed open the door. The little bell rang and I burst into tears.

"I know. Me too. Every time I hear it, I think of Clara," Felix admitted. "Come behind the counter."

I obeyed, putting up no resistance. The smell of coffee mingled with the odor of books hit me. I took a deep breath, in spite of myself. My hand slid along the wooden bar; it was sticky. I picked up a cup; it was dirty; I took another one but that wasn't very clean either.

"Felix, you're fussier about my apartment than you are about Happy People. This is really disgusting."

"It's because I've got too much to do—no time to play housewife," he replied, shrugging his shoulders.

"It's true that it's swarming with people, just like the huge crowds we used to get on our busiest days."

He turned around to help his only customer, with whom he seemed on more than intimate terms, given the way they were ogling each other. The guy finished his drink and left with a book under his arm without bothering to pay.

"So, you're coming back to work?" Felix asked, pouring himself a drink.

"What are you talking about?"

"You've come here because you want to get back to work, right?"

"No, as you know very well. I just want to take some books with me."

"So you're really going? But you've got time, no rush."

"You haven't listened to a thing I've said. I'm leaving in a week; I've already signed and returned the lease agreement."

"What lease agreement?"

"The one for the cottage I'm going to live in for the next few months."

"Are you sure that isn't risky?"

"I'm not sure of anything; I'll see when I get there."

We kept staring at each other.

"Diane, you can't leave me all alone here."

"You've been working away without me for more than a year, and I'm not exactly well known for being efficient. Come on, suggest some books for me."

With no enthusiasm whatsoever, he recommended the books he liked; I agreed without even stopping to think; I couldn't care less. I had already heard of one of them: *Tales of the City*. To my best friend, Armistead Maupin had the power to solve any problem. I knew nothing about it; I'd never read it. Felix piled the books one on top of the other on the counter. He couldn't look at me.

"I'll bring them to your place; they're heavy."

"Thanks. I'll go now; I've got a lot to do."

I glanced over at a little recess behind the bar. I was curious, so I walked towards it. In it stood framed photos of Colin, Clara, Felix, and me. It had been done with great care. I looked back at Felix.

"Go home now," he said softly.

He was standing near the door; I stopped beside him, gave him a gentle kiss on the cheek, and left.

"Diane! I won't be coming over tonight."

"OK. See you tomorrow."

*

"Colin!"

My heart was racing. I was sweating and feeling all around the bed. My only reply was the cold emptiness where he should have been. And yet Colin was with me, he was kissing me, his lips were nibbling at the skin on my neck and had worked their way down from behind my ear to my shoulder. His breath at the back of my neck, the words he whispered, our legs intertwined. I pushed back the sheets and stood barefoot on the parquet floor. The lights of the city lit up the apartment. The sound of the wooden floor creaking as I walked reminded me of Clara's little feet running towards the front door when she heard Colin's keys in the lock.

Every night the same ritual was repeated. We were snuggled up against each other on the sofa. Clara in her nightdress and me eager to see my husband again. I would go into the entrance hall and Colin would have just enough time to put his files down on the table before his little one would jump into his arms.

In the darkness, I followed in their footsteps, into the living room where we would all be together. Colin would come over to me, I'd take off his tie, he would kiss me, Clara would stand between us, we'd have dinner, Colin would put our daughter to sleep, and then we'd be alone together, confident in the knowledge that Clara was safely in her bed, sucking her thumb.

I realized that our apartment no longer existed; I had wanted to stay here to keep everything intact; I was wrong. No more files, no more hearing the sound of keys in the lock, no more racing around on the parquet floor. I would never come back here.

Forty-five minutes on the subway only to end up stuck at the bottom of the stairs to the exit. My legs felt heavier with each step. The cemetery entrance was right near the station, but I didn't know that. Just as I went through the gates, I told myself that I couldn't go empty-handed. I walked to the closest flower shop; there were plenty in the neighborhood.

"I'd like some flowers."

"You're in the right place!" the florist said, smiling. "Is it for a particular occasion?"

"For over there," I said, looking towards the cemetery.

"Do you want something traditional?"

"Just give me two roses, that's all I need."

Surprised, she walked over to the cut flowers.

"White ones," I said. "And don't wrap them up; I'll take them as they are."

"But . . ."

"How much do I owe you?"

I left the money, grabbed the roses from her, and rushed out. My wild race stopped when I got to the gravel lane of the main path. I turned around and around, searching in all directions. Where were they? I went outside again and fell in a heap on the ground. I hurriedly dialed Happy People's number.

"Happy people booze it up and have sex. How can I help you?"

"Felix," I whispered.

"Are you all right?"

"I don't know where they are, can you imagine? I can't even go and see them."

"Who are you trying to see? I don't know what you mean. Where are you? Why are you crying?"

"I want to see Colin and Clara."

"You're at . . . at the cemetery?"

"Yes."

"I'm on my way; don't move."

I'd only been to the cemetery once, the day of the funeral. I'd emphatically refused to go there afterwards.

After running away from the hospital, the day they died, I hadn't set foot there again. Both my parents and Colin's looked horrified when I announced that I wouldn't be there when they put their bodies in the coffins. My in-laws left and slammed the door.

"Diane, you're going completely mad!" my mother exclaimed.

"I can't be there, Mom, it's too hard. If I watch them disappear into those boxes, that would mean it's all over."

"Colin and Clara are dead," she replied. "You have to accept it."

"Be quiet! And I'm not going to the funeral, I don't want to see them go."

I started crying again and turned my back on them.

"What?" my father spat.

"It's your duty," my mother added. "You will go and you won't make a scene."

"My duty? You're talking to me about duty? I couldn't give a damn about that."

I turned angrily towards them. Rage had replaced my grief.

"Well, you do have responsibilities," my father said, "and you will carry them out."

"You don't give a damn about Colin, Clara, or me. All you care about is keeping up appearances, fulfilling the image of a devastated family."

"But that's exactly what we are," my mother retorted.

"No! The only family I've ever known, my only real family, is the one I've just lost."

I could barely breathe anymore; my chest was heaving. I kept staring at them. Their faces contorted for a brief moment. I looked at them for some sign of remorse, but there was none. Their façade was unshakable.

"You have no right to talk to us like that," my father replied. "We're your parents."

"Get out!" I screamed, pointing at the door. "Get the hell out of my house!"

My father walked over to my mother, grabbed

her by the arm, and led her to the door.

"Be ready on time," she said before disappearing. "We'll come and get you."

They returned, as mechanical and exacting as a Swiss clock. They'd listened to nothing I'd said.

In the state of exhaustion I was in, I didn't have the strength to fight. Without the slightest hint of tenderness, my mother forced me to get dressed and my father shoved me into the car. In front of the church, I broke free of them and threw myself into Felix's arms. From that moment on, I stayed with him. When the funeral cars arrived, I hid my face against his chest. Throughout the entire ceremony, he whispered in my ear, telling me about the past few days. He'd chosen the clothes they'd be buried in: Clara's Liberty dress and the soft toy he'd placed next to her, Colin's grey tie and the watch I'd given him for his thirtieth birthday. It was with Felix that I made the journey to the cemetery. I remained in the background until my parents came over to us. They held out some flowers to me.

"Felix, help her to go over there," my father said. "She has to do it. Now isn't the time to be difficult."

Felix squeezed my hand hard and snatched the flowers from my mother.

"Don't do it for your parents, do it for you, for Colin and Clara."

I threw the flowers into the hole in the ground.

"I came as fast as I could," Felix said when he found me. "Let go of the roses, you're hurting yourself."

He crouched down beside me, opened my fingers one by one, took the roses and put them on the ground. My hands were bleeding; I hadn't even felt the stinging thorns. He put an arm around my waist and helped me stand up.

We walked through the cemetery until we came to a water fountain. He washed my hands without saying a word. He took a watering can and filled it up. He led me along by his side, knowing exactly where he was going. He let go of me and started to clean a tombstone, their tombstone, the tombstone I was seeing for the first time. I took in every detail: the color of the marble, the calligraphy used to carve their names. Colin had lived for thirty-three years and Clara hadn't even had the chance to celebrate her sixth birthday. Felix handed me the two roses.

"Talk to them."

I put my ridiculous present on the tombstone and fell to my knees.

"Well, my loves . . . forgive me . . . I don't know what to say to you . . ."

My voice broke. I buried my face in my hands. I was cold. And hot. I was in pain.

"It's so hard. Colin, why did you take Clara with you? You had no right to leave, no right to take her with you. The only thing I hold against you is that you left me all alone. I'm lost. I should have died with you both."

I wiped away my tears with the back of my hand. I sniffled noisily.

"I just can't believe you're never coming back. I spend my whole life waiting for you. Everything is ready for you at home . . . People tell me it isn't normal. So I'm going away. You remember how you wanted to go to Ireland, Colin, and I said no; I was stupid . . . I'm going to go there for a while. I don't know where you are, the two of you, but I need you, watch over me, protect me. I love you . . ."

I closed my eyes for a few seconds. Then I got up with great difficulty; I couldn't get my balance and my head was spinning; Felix helped me steady myself. We headed for the exit without looking back and without saying a word. Before going down to the subway, Felix stopped.

"You know, until now I didn't believe you when you said you wanted to get better," he admitted, "but what you did today proves I was wrong. I'm proud of you."

I waited until the day before my departure to call my parents. Ever since I'd told them my decision, they hadn't stopped trying to convince me to stay. They called me every day and my answering machine worked wonderfully.

"Mom, it's Diane."

In the background was the usual sound of the television with the volume turned up as loud as possible.

"How are you, my darling?"

"I'm ready to leave."

"The same old song! It's your daughter, my dear, she still wants to go away."

A chair creaked on the tiled floor and my father took the receiver.

"Listen, my girl, you're going to come and spend a few days with us and that will get you thinking straight again."

"Dad, that wouldn't do any good. I'm leaving tomorrow. You still haven't understood that I don't want to come back and live with you. I'm a big girl and you don't live with your parents when you're thirty-two."

"You've never known how to manage by yourself. You need someone to guide you; you're incapable of seeing a plan through. The facts speak for themselves. We supported you and if you have enough to live on now and carry through this absurd idea it's only because Colin had some foresight. So frankly, going abroad is way beyond your capabilities."

"Thanks Dad, I didn't know I was such a ball and chain around your neck. I'll make sure to think about what you said when I need cheering up."

"Let me speak to her," my mother said in the background. "You're getting her back up." She took the phone again. "Your father isn't very diplomatic, my darling, but he's right. You don't think things through. Now if Felix were going with you, we'd feel better, even if he isn't the ideal person to take care of you. Listen, we've left you alone up until now, thinking you'd get better with time. Why didn't you go and see the psychiatrist I talked to you about? It would do you good."

"Mom, that's enough. I don't want a shrink, I don't want to live with you, and I don't want Felix to go with me. I want peace, I want to be alone, and I'm fed up with being watched over, you understand? If you want to reach me, you know my cell phone number. And please don't tell me to have a good trip."

Eyes wide open, I stared at the ceiling. I was waiting for my alarm clock to ring. I hadn't slept all night, and the fact that I'd hung up on my parents had nothing to do with my insomnia. In a few hours I'd be getting on a plane, headed to Ireland. I had just spent my last night in our apartment, in our bed.

One last time, I snuggled up against Colin's side of the bed, my head buried in his pillow, and cuddled Clara's favorite soft toy; my tears made them damp. The alarm clock went off and I got out of bed, like a robot.

In the bathroom, I uncovered the mirror and saw myself for the first time in months. Swamped in Colin's shirt. I watched my fingers open each button; one shoulder was freed, then the other. The shirt fell from my body onto the floor. I washed my hair one last time with Clara's shampoo. When I got out of the shower, I avoided looking at the shirt on the floor. I dressed myself as Diane, in jeans, a sleeveless T-shirt, and a tight-fitting sweater. Immediately I felt like I was suffocating; I struggled to get the sweater off and grabbed Colin's hoodie. I put it on and could breathe again. I'd worn it often before his death, so I gave myself the right to wear it now.

I glanced at my watch and saw I had very little time left. A coffee in my hand and a cigarette between my lips, I chose a few framed photos at random from the living room and slipped them into my bag.

I sat on the sofa waiting until it was time to go, nervously wringing my hands; my thumb hit my wedding ring. I would surely encounter people in

Ireland and they would see that I was married; they'd ask me where my husband was and I wouldn't be able to answer. I couldn't be without my ring so I had to hide it. I opened the chain of the necklace I was wearing, slipped the ring on it, and put it back on, hiding it under my sweatshirt.

Two rings at the doorbell broke the silence. The door opened to reveal Felix. He came in without saying a word and looked deep into my eyes. His face bore witness to the excesses of the previous night. His eyes were red and swollen. He reeked of alcohol and tobacco. He didn't have to say a word for me to know his voice was hoarse. He started taking down my bags. There were a lot of them. I walked around the apartment, turned off all the lights, closed the doors to all the rooms. My hand tensed on the handle of the front door as I closed it. The only sound was the click of the lock.

3

I stood in front of the rental car with my suitcases at my feet, my arms hanging down at my sides, holding the keys. Great gusts of wind swirled around the parking lot, making me lose my balance.

Ever since I'd left the airplane, I felt like I was drifting. I'd automatically followed the other passengers to the moving walkway to pick up my bags. Then a little later, at the car rental agency, I'd managed to understand the person I was talking to—in spite of his accent that you could cut with a knife—and I'd signed the contract.

But now, standing in front of the car, freezing cold, aching all over, exhausted, I wondered what kind of a mess I'd gotten myself into. I had no choice, I wanted to have a home, and from now on, home was going to be Mulranny.

I had to try several times before I could light a cigarette. The biting wind never died down and it was already starting to get on my nerves. It was even worse when I realized it was burning my ciggy down. I lit up another one before loading up the trunk. Then there was a powerful gust of wind and I set fire to a few strands of my hair that flew into my face.

A sticker on the windshield reminded me that here you drive on the left. I started the engine, put the car in first and the car stalled. My second and third attempt to get it started also failed. I'd been given a lemon. I walked over to the office where there were five strong young guys. They were smiling; they'd seen the whole thing.

"I'd like you to change my car," I said, annoyed. "It doesn't work."

"Hello," the oldest one replied, still smiling. "What's wrong?"

"I have no idea. It won't start."

"Come on, boys. Let's help the little lady."

I stood back while they went outside, impressed by their size. "Rugby players and mutton eaters," Felix had said. He wasn't wrong. They walked me to the car. I tried to start the car but no luck. It stalled again.

"You're in the wrong gear," one of the giants told me, laughing out loud.

"No I'm not . . . not at all. I do know how to drive."

"Put it into fifth, what you think is fifth, and you'll see."

He was looking at me but he wasn't mocking me any more. I did what he said. The car started.

"Everything's backwards here. The side of the road you drive on, the steering wheel, the gears."

"Are you all right now?" one of the others asked.

"Yes. Thank you."

"Where are you headed?"

"Mulranny."

"That's a way off. Be careful and take care at the traffic circles."

"Thank you very much."

"A pleasure. Goodbye, have a good trip."

They nodded to me and gave me a big smile. Since when were guys who rented cars so friendly and helpful?

I was halfway there and just starting to relax. I'd successfully passed the test of the highway and the first traffic circle. Nothing special along the way except some sheep and shimmering green fields. As far as the eye could see. No traffic jams, no rain on the horizon.

Saying goodbye to Felix went round and round in my mind. We hadn't exchanged a single word between my place and the airport. He'd smoked one cigarette after the other without looking at me. He only spoke at the very last minute. We were standing opposite each other, looking at each other and hesitating.

"You'll take care of yourself?" he asked.

"Don't worry."

"You can still change your mind, you don't have to go."

"Don't make this more difficult. It's time. I have to board now."

I've never been able to stand goodbyes. Leaving him was more difficult than I'd imagined. I crushed myself against him; he took a few seconds to react, then held me in his arms.

"Take care of yourself," I said. "Don't do anything stupid. Promise?"

"We'll see. Get going now."

He let go of me. I picked up my bag and walked towards security. I gave him a little wave. Then I took out my passport. I could feel Felix watching me throughout the whole process. But I didn't look back once.

I was here. I was in Mulranny. In front of the cottage whose photos I'd hardly looked at on the ad. I had to drive through the entire village and take the twisting road along the beach to get to my house.

I'd have neighbors. Another house was next to mine, a few yards away. As I tried to decide how I felt about neighbors, a tiny little woman in her mid-sixties came pedaling up the road on a bicycle. She dismounted and came towards me with a wave. I forced myself to smile.

"Hello, Diane. I'm Abby, your landlady. Did you have a good trip?"

"Very pleased to meet you."

She looked at the hand I stretched out to her with amusement, then shook hands.

"You know, everyone here knows each other. And you're not on a job interview. Please don't get it into your head to call me Madam all the time. Same goes when it comes to consideration and good manners, OK?"

She invited me into the place that was to become my home. I found it warm and cozy inside.

Abby never stopped talking; I only listened to half of what she said, nodding in reply with a dumb smile on my face. She treated me to a description of all the appliances in the kitchen, the cable channels, the times when it was high tide, and when Mass was held, of course. That was when I cut in.

"I don't think I'll be needing that, I have no interest in the Church."

"Then we have a serious problem, Diane. You should have done some research before coming here. We fought for our independence and our religion.

You're going to be living with Irish Catholics who are proud of it."

This was turning out to be a good start.

"Abby, I'm very sorry, I . . ."

She burst out laughing.

"Relax, for Heaven's sake! It was a joke. It's just how I am. There's no obligation to go with me on Sunday mornings. On the other hand, one piece of advice: never forget that we're Irish, not English."

"I'll remember that."

She quickly continued her guided tour. Upstairs, my bathroom and bedroom. I'd be able to lie sideways across my bed; it was an extra-large king size. Normal in the land of giants.

"Abby," I cut in, "thank you. It's perfect. I have everything I'll need."

"Forgive my enthusiasm, but I'm so happy that someone is going to live in the cottage during the winter; I've really been looking forward to having you here. I'll let you get settled in."

I walked her out. She climbed onto her bike and turned towards me.

"Come and have a coffee with us. We're on the

other end of Mulranny; you have my address. You'll meet Jack."

On my first night, as a welcome gesture, a storm broke out. The wind raged, rain lashed against the windows, the roof creaked. Impossible to get to sleep in spite of my weariness and the comfortable bed. I thought back about the day I'd had.

Emptying my car was even more of a task than loading it up; my suitcases were scattered all over the living room. I'd been this close to giving up when I'd realized I had nothing to eat. I hurried into the little kitchen. The cabinets and fridge were full to bursting. Abby surely must have told me and I hadn't thanked her. Shameful. How rude of me. I'd certainly run into her some day to apologize. As she'd said, Mulranny was a really small place: one main street, a mini-market, a gas station, and a pub. There was no chance I'd get lost or burn out my credit card in the boutiques.

The welcome I'd received from my landlady left me puzzled. She seemed to expect some kind of close relationship, which wasn't at all what I had envisaged. I would put off accepting her invitation as long as I could; I wasn't here to keep an old couple company and I didn't want to get to know anyone.

I held out for a week without leaving the cottage; Abby's supplies and the cartons of cigarettes I'd brought had kept me going. It had also taken all that time to unpack everything. It was difficult to feel at home; nothing reminded me of my former life. Streetlamps didn't light up the night and there were none of the noises you hear in the city. When the wind died down, the silence became oppressive. I wished that my neighbors (still away) would hold a big party so the sound would lull me to sleep. The heady aroma of the potpourri was totally different from the smell of the polished parquet floor in our apartment, and the anonymity of the Parisian shop-keepers was definitely very far away.

I was beginning to regret not having gone out earlier; perhaps I would have avoided everyone staring at me when I went into the mini-market. No need to try to work out what people were saying. Everyone was talking about me—the stranger, the foreigner. The customers turned towards me as I walked past, smiling and nodding at me. A few of them spoke to me. I mumbled some reply. It wasn't part of my routine to say hello to people I came across in the stores. I slowly walked around the aisles. There was a bit of everything, food, clothes, even souvenirs for tourists. Though I must have been the only madwoman to risk coming here. One thing was a permanent feature: there was stewing mutton on the butcher's shelves and sheep everywhere, on china cups and in the knitted sweaters and scarves, of course. Here, they raised these little animals for food and clothing. Like they did with mammoths in prehistoric times.

A hand fell on my arm. "Diane. I'm so happy to run into you," said Abby. I hadn't seen her come in.

I was startled, then said, "Hello."

"I was thinking of stopping by today. Is everything all right?"

"Yes, thank you."

"Have you found everything you need?"

"Not really, they don't have everything I'm looking for."

"You mean your baguette and cheese?"

"Uh . . . I . . ."

"Hey, I'm just teasing you. Are you done now?"

"I think so."

"Come with me; I'll introduce you."

With a dazzling smile on her face, she grabbed hold of my arm and took me to meet everyone. I hadn't spoken to so many people in months. Their kindness was almost disturbing. After half an hour of small talk, I finally managed to make my way to the register. I could lock myself away for at least ten days with all of the supplies I'd purchased. Except that I was going to have to go out since I couldn't find an excuse to refuse Abby's invitation; I'd simply negotiated a few days to prepare myself.

My landlords had a nice home. I was comfortably settled on the couch, in front of a large fireplace, with a steaming hot cup of tea in my hand.

Jack was a giant with a white beard. His calm demeanor tempered his wife's permanent liveliness. With disconcerting ease, he had poured himself a pint of Guinness at four o'clock in the afternoon.

Rugby players who eat mutton and drink stout, I mused, to complete Felix's description. And the dark ale immediately made me think of Colin.

In spite of this, I managed to hold up my end of the conversation. I first talked about their dog, Postman Pat, who had jumped all over me when I arrived and who never left my side. Then I talked about the rain and the nice weather—well, mainly about the rain—and how comfortable the cottage was. After that, I started to run out of things to say.

"Are you from Mulranny?" I finally asked.

"Yes, but we lived in Dublin until I retired," Jack replied.

"What did you do?"

"He was a doctor," Abby cut in. "But tell us what you do, that's far more interesting. And I'm especially curious to know why you would come to bury yourself in this place."

Bury myself, exactly; the answer was in the question.

"I wanted to see some new places."

"All alone? How come a pretty girl like you isn't with someone?"

"Leave her be," Jack scolded.

"It would take too long to explain. Well, I have to get going," I said, stony-faced.

I stood up, picked up my jacket and handbag and headed to the door. Abby and Jack followed behind. I'd put a damper on things. I tripped over Postman Pat several times, then he ran outside as soon as the door was opened.

"Such a big baby must keep you very busy!" I said (and then thought of Clara).

"Oh, Good Lord, he's not ours," Abby told me.

"Who does he belong to?"

"Edward. Our nephew. We take care of him when Edward's away."

"He's your neighbor."

I was disappointed. I'd thought that the house next door would remain empty, which suited me down to the ground. I didn't need any neighbors. I already felt that my landlords were too close by.

They walked me to my car. The dog started to bark and run around in circles. A black Land Rover spattered with mud had just parked in front of the house, rolling to a halt in front of my car.

"Well, speak of the devil," Jack exclaimed.

"Wait a few minutes," said Abby, taking my arm to hold me back. "We'll introduce you."

The nephew in question got out of the car. His rugged face and scornful expression made me feel no warmth towards him. Jack and Abby went over to him. He leaned against his car's door and crossed his arms. The more I looked at him, the more unappealing I found him. He didn't smile. He reeked of arrogance. The kind of guy who would spend hours in the bathroom to work on looking like a nonchalant adventurer. He made it clear he didn't want to socialize.

"Edward, that's good timing!" Abby said.

"Oh? Why?"

"It's time you met Diane."

He finally turned to look at me. He lowered his sunglasses—useless given the mist—and looked me up and down. I had the impression of being a slab of meat on a counter. And judging from the look he gave me, I didn't seem to stimulate his appetite.

"Um, no, not really. Who is she?" he asked, coldly.

I took it upon myself to remain polite and walked over to him.

"It seems you're my neighbor."

His face clouded over even more. He stood up straight and turned to my hosts, as if I wasn't there.

"I told you I didn't want anyone next door. How long is she staying?"

I tapped him on the back as if it were a door. His whole body stiffened. He turned around but I didn't back off; I stood on tiptoe.

"You can talk to me directly, you know."

He raised one eyebrow, visibly annoyed that I dared speak to him.

"Don't come knocking at my door," he replied, shooting me a look that sent a shiver running through me.

Without any more ado, he turned around, whistled for his dog and went into the back garden.

"Don't you worry about him," Jack said.

"He didn't want us to rent out the cottage but it wasn't any of his business," Abby added. "He's just in a bad mood."

"No, he just hasn't been taught any manners," I muttered. "See you soon."

My car was blocked in by my neighbor's car. I

leaned on the horn without stopping. Abby and Jack burst out laughing before going inside.

I saw Edward arrive in my rearview mirror. He walked over nonchalantly while smoking a cigarette. He opened the Rover's back door and let his dog jump in. His deliberate slowness exasperated me; I tapped on the steering wheel. Without looking in my direction, he flicked his cigarette butt onto my windshield. His tires screeched as he took off, and a wave of muddy water hit my car. By the time I'd put on the windshield wipers, he was gone. The bastard.

I had to find a way to avoid getting soaked every time I left the house to get some air. I got caught in the rain again today. First decision, forget using an umbrella, totally pointless since I'd broken four in four days. Second decision, no longer count on the sunshine: it disappeared as quickly as it arrived. Third and final decision, be prepared to go out when it rained, for by the time I'd put on my boots, three sweaters, my coat and a scarf, the rain might have passed, and I would reduce the chance of getting wet. I'd try it out the next time I felt like going out.

My method worked. That's what I told myself the first time I sat down on the sand to gaze at the sea. Chance had led me to a good spot; it was if I were alone in the world. I closed my eyes, cradled by the sound of the waves that swept over the beach a few yards away. The wind whipped my skin, bringing tears to my eyes, and my lungs filled with the salty sea air.

Suddenly, I was knocked backwards. I opened my eyes to find myself staring at Postman Pat; he was licking my face. I had the greatest difficulty in getting up. I was trying to brush off the sand that covered my clothes when the dog took off to the sound of a whistle.

I looked up. Edward was walking a little farther away. He'd obviously had to pass quite close to me, but he hadn't stopped to say hello. It wasn't possible that he hadn't recognized me. But even if that were the case, anyone whose dog had just jumped on someone would have the manners to come and apologize. I headed for home, having decided to truly tell him off. At the end of the path that led to the cottages, I saw his Land Rover driving towards the village. He wasn't going to get off so lightly.

I climbed into my car. I had to find that oaf and make him understand exactly who he was dealing with. I very quickly found his muddy heap parked in front of the pub. I slammed on the brakes, jumped out of the car, and went into the bar like a Fury. I glanced around the room to find my target. Everyone was looking at me. Except for one.

Yet Edward was there all right, sitting at the counter, alone, leaning over a newspaper, holding a pint of Guinness. I headed straight for him.

"Just who do you think you are?"

No response.

"Look at me when I'm talking to you."

He turned the page of his newspaper.

"Didn't your parents teach you any manners? No one has ever treated me this way and you'd better apologize right now."

I could feel myself turning redder and redder with anger. He still didn't deign to look up from his stupid paper.

"That's enough!" I shouted, grabbing the newspaper from his hands.

He took a drink of beer, put the pint down and sighed deeply. He clenched his fist so tightly that one of his veins stood out. He stood up and stared straight at me. I wondered if I hadn't perhaps gone too far. He grabbed a pack of cigarettes from the counter and headed for the smoking area, a terrace out back. He shook a few people's hands as he walked by without ever saying a word or even smiling.

The door to the terrace slammed shut. I'd been holding my breath since he'd stood up. The whole pub was silent; the entire male population always met there and had all witnessed the scene. I slumped onto the nearest barstool. Someone had to teach him a lesson sometime or other. The bartender shrugged his shoulders and glanced over at me.

"Can I have an espresso, please?" I asked.

"We ain't got that here."

"You don't have any coffee?"

"Sure we do."

I'd have to work on my accent.

"Well then, I'd like to have one, please."

He smiled and went into a corner of the bar. He put a mug down in front of me: it had filtered, watery coffee in it. So much for my idea of good coffee. I didn't understand why the bartender was still standing in front of me.

"Are you going to watch me drink it?"

"I just want to get paid."

"Don't worry. I intend to pay before I leave."

"Here we pay before we start drinking. The English idea of service."

"OK, OK."

I handed him the money and he gave me my change in a friendly way. Prepared to burn my mouth, I quickly drank my coffee and left. What a strange country: everyone was so nice and welcoming, with the exception of that brute Edward, but you had to pay for your drinks right away. In Paris, that charming bartender would have been put in his place before he knew it. Except that in France, the same bartender wouldn't have been friendly, he wouldn't have chatted to you, and as for cracking a smile, dream on.

*

I'd gone back to my old ways. I didn't get dressed anymore, ate whatever was around, whenever I felt like it. I slept for a good part of the day. If I couldn't fall asleep, I stayed in bed watching the sky and the clouds, nice and warm under my duvet. I sat comatose in front of inane TV shows, which turned into silent movies when they were in Gaelic. I talked to Colin and Clara, staring at their photos. I was living as I had in our apartment, in Paris, but without Felix. And yet, the sense of comfort I desperately longed for remained out of reach. The heaviness in my heart did not diminish; I felt in no way liberated. I didn't want to do anything, I couldn't even cry any more. Time passed, and the days seemed to grow longer and longer.

One morning, instead of staying in bed, I decided to bury myself in the large armchair that looked out onto the beach. After days of staring at the sky, I was going to amuse myself by watching the sea. I gathered together my stock of coffee and cigarettes, wrapped myself in a robe and shoved a cushion behind my head.

The sound of barking broke through my haze. Edward and his dog were going out. It was the first time I'd seen my neighbor since the incident in the pub. He had a large bag over his shoulder. To see what he was doing better, I moved my armchair closer to the window. He was headed to the beach. His brown hair was even messier than before.

He disappeared from sight when he went behind a rock. He reappeared half an hour later, put his bag down and started looking for something inside. I would have needed binoculars to know what he was fiddling with. He crouched down; all I could see was his back. He stayed in the same position for a long time.

My stomach was growling, which reminded me that I hadn't eaten anything since the day before. I went into the kitchen to make myself a sandwich. When I got back into the living room, Edward had gone. My only entertainment for the day was over. I curled up in the armchair and ate my snack, but I had no appetite.

Hours passed; I didn't move. I stirred when I saw the lights go out at Edward's house. He ran outside to go to exactly the same place he'd been that morning. I pulled my robe tighter around my shoulders and went out onto the porch to see him better. I could tell he was holding something in his hands. He held it up to his face and I thought I could make out a camera.

Edward stayed there for a good hour, and I watched him the whole time. Night had fallen when he came back from the beach. I just had enough time to crouch down so he wouldn't see me. I waited a few minutes before going back inside.

My neighbor was a photographer. For the past week I'd synchronized my days with his. He came out at different times, always with his camera. He paced up and down the entire bay of Mulranny. He could remain still for hours at a time and never reacted to the rain or wind that sometimes battered him.

Thanks to my stakeout, I'd learned a lot. He was even more of an addict than I was: he smoked constantly. His appearance, on the day we first met, was in no way exceptional; he was always unkempt. He never spoke to anyone, never had anyone over to his house. I'd never seen him glance in my direction. Conclusion: this guy was completely self-centered.

He gave no thought to anything or anyone, apart from his photos—always the same wave, always the same sand. He was very predictable; I didn't need to wonder where he was for long. Depending on what time it was, he would be at one rock or the other.

One morning, I hadn't looked out the window to check he was there. But the more time that passed, the stranger I found it that I couldn't even hear his dog barking, because he followed him everywhere. To my great surprise, I saw that his Land Rover was gone. Suddenly, I thought of Felix; I hadn't called him since I'd left, a month and a half ago; it was time. I grabbed my cell phone and found his number in the contacts.

"Felix, it's Diane," I said, when he picked up.

"Don't know her."

He hung up on me. I called back.

"Felix, don't hang up."

"So you finally remembered me?"

"I'm an idiot, I know. Sorry."

"When are you coming back?"

"I'm not. I'm staying in Ireland."

"You're having a ball in your new life?"

I told him that my landlords were charming, that I'd had supper with them several times, that all the locals welcomed me with open arms, that I regularly went for a drink at the pub. The sound of an engine stopped my enthusiasm.

"Diane, are you there?"

"Yes, give me a minute please."

"Has someone come to see you?"

"No, my neighbor's come home."

"You have a neighbor?"

"Yes, and I could happily do without him."

I started telling him about Edward, the details tumbling out in a rush.

"Diane, could you please pause for breath?"

"Sorry, but this guy really gets on my nerves. What's new with you?"

"It's pretty quiet at the moment; I don't open the bookshop until early evening, and it's not going too badly, there's some money coming in. I've organized an evening on the most famous debauched characters in literature."

"You're kidding."

"I can guarantee that if anyone writes a book

about me, I'll win the prize. Ever since you left, I have more time and I'm having a ball, my evenings are incredible and my nights steaming hot. Your chaste little ears wouldn't be able to stand hearing about it."

As I hung up, three things were clear to me: Felix would never change, I missed him, and my neighbor didn't deserve a second thought. I quickly pulled the curtains closed.

It was October. I made an effort to try to start reading again. But that afternoon, it gave me no solace. I didn't know if it was because of the dreary detective novel by Arnaldur Indridason I'd gotten stuck into, or the draft I felt on my back. My hands were frozen. The cottage was even more silent than usual. I stood up, rubbed my arms to warm them up, and stopped for a moment in front of the bay window; the weather was bad. Heavy clouds blocked out the sky; night would fall earlier tonight. I regretted not knowing how to light a fire. When I touched one of the radiators, I was surprised; it wasn't hot. I would die of the cold if the heating was broken. I wanted to turn on a light. The first lamp remained hopelessly dark. I flicked on a different switch with the same result. I tried all the switches. No electricity. Total darkness. And me inside. All alone.

Even though it cost me dearly, I ran and banged on Edward's door. I knocked so hard on the wooden door that I ended up hurting my hand. I moved back a little to try to look through a window. If I had to be alone for even one more minute, I'd go mad. I heard some funny noises behind me and was afraid.

"Can you tell me what you're doing?" someone asked behind me.

I turned around quickly. Edward was looming over me at full height. I stepped aside to get away from him. My fear became totally irrational.

"I made a mistake . . . I . . . I . . ."

"You did what?"

"I shouldn't have come. I won't bother you again."

Still watching him, I started backing away onto the road. My heel hit a stone and I found myself flat on my back, my butt in the mud. Edward walked over to me. His look was sour but he reached his hand out to me.

"Don't touch me."

He raised one eyebrow and stood still.

"Just my luck to run into a crazy Frenchwoman."

I got myself onto all fours to stand up. I could hear Edward's bitter laughter. I ran to my house and double-locked the door to barricade myself in. Then I took refuge in my bed.

In spite of the blankets and my sweaters, I was shivering. I squeezed my wedding ring tightly. It was pitch black. I was afraid. I was sobbing so hard I could barely breathe. I curled up in a ball. My back ached because I was trying to curl up tightly to fight the shivers. I bit my pillow to stop myself from screaming.

I drifted in and out of sleep. The electricity didn't miraculously come back on during the night. I turned to the only person who could help me, even if it was only by phone.

"Shit, some people are asleep," Felix shouted. It was the second time I'd called him in the past 24 hours.

"I'm sorry," I said and started to cry again.

"What's happened?"

"I'm cold, I'm in the dark."

"What?"

"I haven't had any electricity since yesterday afternoon."

"And you couldn't find anyone to help you?"

"I went to my neighbor's, but I didn't dare disturb him."

"Why not?"

"I think he might be a serial killer."

"Have you been smoking sheep's wool?"

"I don't have any electricity, help me."

"Did you check to see if a fuse blew?"

"No."

"Go and see."

I listened to Felix. My cell phone still glued to my ear, I went and reset the fuse box. All the lights and the appliances came on.

"Well?" Felix asked.

"It worked, thank you."

"You're sure you're OK?"

"Yes, go back to sleep. I'm really sorry."

I hung up right away. I slumped down on the ground. I was definitely incapable of solving the smallest problem without someone's help; my parents were right. I felt like slapping myself.

4

I'd forgotten what it felt like to listen to music that was so loud my eardrums nearly burst. I'd hesitated a long time before turning on the hi-fi, remembering there was a time when I did it without thinking. I kept glancing at it, hesitating, pacing up and down all around it.

The incident of the fuse box had shaken up my routine. I forced myself to go out more often. I went for little walks on the beach. I tried not to drag myself around in my pajamas all day long. I did everything to get back to the world of the living and stop wallowing in paranoid delusions. One morning, I surprised myself when I felt less despondent when I woke up; I'd felt like hearing music and I'd listened to some. Of course I cried; my euphoria hadn't lasted.

The next day, I put the music on again. Then I couldn't help but move along to it in time. I was getting back in touch with old habits. I danced like a madwoman all alone in my living room. The only difference in Mulranny was that I didn't need earphones; I danced to my heart's content, the bass pounding.

"*The dog days are over, the dog days are done. Can you hear the horses? 'Cause here they come.*" I shared the stage with Florence and the Machine. I knew this song by heart; I never missed a beat. I twisted and turned. A fine layer of sweat covered my skin, I flung my ponytail all over the place and my cheeks were bright red, of course. Suddenly, one sound seemed out of place. I turned down the volume but still heard the same racket. I walked over to the door with the remote still in my hand. The door was shaking. I counted to three before opening it.

"Hello, Edward. What can I do for you?" I asked with my sweetest smile.

"Turn down your damned music!"

"Don't you like English rock? They're your compatriots . . ."

He banged on the doorframe.

"I'm not English."

"That's obvious. You don't have their famous stiff upper lip."

I continued smiling brightly. He clenched and unclenched his fists, closed his eyes, and took a deep breath.

"You're asking for it from me," he said in his hoarse voice.

"Not at all. You're actually the opposite of what I'd ask for."

"Be careful."

"Ooh, I'm scared."

He pointed a finger at me and clenched his teeth.

"I'm just asking you to turn it down. It's making my darkroom vibrate and it's disturbing me."

I burst out laughing.

"So you're really a photographer?"

"What business is that of yours?"

"None at all. But you must be really bad at it."

If I were a man, he would have hit me.

"Photography is an art," I continued, "which requires a minimum of sensitivity. But you have absolutely none. So my conclusion is that you weren't made for that profession. Well, listen, it's been awfully nice talking to you . . . No, I'm kidding, so excuse me, I have better things to do."

I gave him a look of defiance, pointed the remote at the hi-fi, and turned it up as loud as it would go. *"Happiness hit her like a bullet in the head. Struck from a great height by someone who should know better than that. The dog days are over, the dog days are done,"* I howled, then writhed about in front of him before slamming the door in his face.

I felt elated as I danced, singing at the top of my lungs. It felt so good to have shut him up! I really wanted to keep the game going and finish what I'd started; I decided I was going to ruin his whole day. He was obviously the kind of guy who would go and have a drink to calm down. So I picked up my keys and headed to the pub.

Unlike the first time, I went into the pub in a civilized manner. I greeted everyone with a wave of the hand and added a smile. I ordered a glass of red wine and paid for my drink right away, then sat down at a respectable distance from my neighbor.

He was scowling even more than usual; I must have really got on his nerves. He was fiddling with his lighter, his jaw clenched. He drank his first beer all at once, then ordered another with a nod of the head. He stared at me. I raised my glass to him and took a sip. It was all I could do not to spit it out. The wine, if you could really call it that, was undrinkable. A knowledgeable wine merchant would have sooner recommended a cheap local wine in a plastic bottle. What was I thinking? That I'd be served a good vintage wine in this godforsaken Irish hole where no one drank anything but Guinness and whisky? Still, it didn't stop me looking defiantly at Edward.

This little game lasted a good half an hour. I finally won when he stood up and headed for the door. I'd just won a battle; I had accomplished something that day.

I waited a few minutes before leaving. Night had fallen; I pulled up the collar of my coat. It was the end of October and you could feel the first signs of winter coming on.

"Just as I thought," a hoarse voice said.

Edward was waiting for me next to my car. He was alarmingly quiet.

"I thought you'd gone home. Don't you have any pictures to develop?"

"You made me ruin a whole roll of film today, so don't talk to me about my work. You probably don't even know what it means to work."

Without giving me a chance to reply, he kept talking.

"I don't need to know you to see that you do nothing all day long. Don't you have any family or friends who want you to get back?"

Fear made me stammer; he was back in control.

"No, obviously not! Who'd want anything to do with you? There's nothing interesting about you. You must have had a guy, but I bet he died of boredom . . ."

My hand flew up by itself. I hit him so hard that

HAPPY PEOPLE READ & DRINK COFFEE

his head fell to the side. He rubbed his cheek and smirked.

"So I've hit a nerve?"

I was breathing more quickly; tears came to my eyes.

"I see. He didn't want anything to do with you any more. He was right to dump you."

He was blocking my car.

"Get out of my way," I said.

He grabbed my arm to hold me back and stared straight into my eyes.

"Don't ever do that again. And get yourself a ticket home."

He angrily let go of me and disappeared into the night. I wiped away my tears with the back of my hand. I was shaking so hard that I dropped my keys. I was still desperately trying to open my car door when Edward sped away. Without actually being a murderer, that man was dangerous.

I was sitting on the floor in the middle of the living room. A dim light filled the room. The first bottle of wine was almost finished. Before putting out my cigarette, I used what was left of it to light the next one. I finally picked up my phone.

"Felix, it's me."

"What's new in the land of sheep?"

"I can't stand it any more; I've had enough."

"What are you saying?"

"I've tried, I promise, I've forced myself but it's not working."

"It will get better," he said softly.

"No! It will never get better; there's nothing left, nothing at all."

"It's normal that you feel bad around now. Clara's birthday brings up too many memories."

"You'll go and see her tomorrow?"

"Yes, I'm taking care of her . . . Come home."

"Good night."

I staggered into the kitchen. I gave up on the wine. I drowned some orange juice in rum, a glass in one hand, the bottle in the other, and continued my breakdown. I drank, smoked, and cried until dawn.

It was daybreak when my insides started to turn. I ran up to the bathroom without caring what I knocked over. My body was wracked with spasms, each more violent than the next. After vomiting for what felt like hours, I dragged myself into the shower without even bothering to undress. I sat down under the water, my knees bent, rocking back and forth and wailing. The hot water grew warm, then cool then icy cold.

My soaking wet things sat on the bathroom tiles. My clean, dry clothes didn't make me feel any better, not even Colin's sweatshirt. I was suffocating. I put the hood up and went out just as storm clouds were rolling in.

My legs managed to get me to the beach. Lying on the shore, I stared at the raging sea; the rain hammered against my face; the wind and rain stung me. I wanted to go to sleep, forever, it didn't matter where. My place was with Colin and Clara; I'd found a good spot to join them. I was lost in a state between dream and reality. Little by little, I stopped thinking. My arms and legs grew heavy with cold; I sank deeper and deeper. It was getting darker and darker. The storm helped me to drift away.

A dog barked close by. I could feel him sniffing me, nuzzling against me to make me react. As soon as he heard a whistle, he ran off. I would be able to end my journey.

"What are you doing here?"

I recognized Edward's hoarse voice and fear ran through me. I tried to huddle up in a ball, closed my eyes as tightly as I could, and put one hand on my head to protect myself.

"Leave me the hell alone!" I muttered. I could feel his hands on me, like an electric shock. I fought, kicking and beating him with my fists.

"Let go of me!"

I managed to break free. I tried to stand up but I was just too weak. I was about to fall when the ground gave way. I was trapped in Edward's arms.

"Be quiet and let me help you."

I couldn't fight any more. I instinctively put my arms around his neck. His body protected me from the raging wind. The rain stopped; we were inside somewhere. Without putting me down, he went up some stairs. He pushed the door open with his shoulder, then went into the room and put me down on a bed. My head was down and I was hunched over. Without looking directly at him, I saw him throw his jacket into a corner of the room. He disappeared for a few minutes before coming back, one towel around his neck and the other in his hand. He kneeled down in front of me and started drying my forehead and cheeks. He had large hands. He pulled my hood back and untied my hair.

"Take off your sweater."

"No," I replied, shaking my head, my voice breaking.

"You have no choice; if you don't get out of those clothes, you'll get sick."

"I can't."

I was shivering harder and harder. He leaned down and took off my boots and socks.

"Stand up."

I held on to the bed to steady myself. Edward took Colin's sweatshirt off me. I lost my balance; he caught me by the waist and held me against him for a few seconds before letting me go. He unbuttoned my jeans and pulled them down. He held me up so I could take them off. His hands brushed against my back when he took off my T-shirt. A fit of modesty made me cross my arms over my chest. He went to rifle through a closet and came back with a shirt, then helped me put it on. Memories rose up at the same time as my tears. Edward closed all the buttons and slipped my wedding ring inside the shirt.

"Lie down."

I stretched out on the bed and he pulled the duvet over me. He pushed the hair off my face. I sensed him moving away. I was breathing through my sobs and crying even harder. I opened my eyes and looked at him for the first time. He wiped his face with his hand and went out. I took my wedding ring from under the shirt and held it tightly. I curled up in a fetal position and buried my head in the pillow. Then I finally sank into a deep sleep.

I didn't want to get up, yet my senses were awake. My eyes were twitching. The walls of my bedroom weren't gray, they were white. I reached out to switch on my bedside lamp but there was nothing there. I jumped up, sat down on the bed and found I had a blinding headache. I massaged my temples and in a flash, remembered what had happened the day before. But as for what had happened during the night, that was a complete blank.

I took my first steps hesitantly. I pressed my ear against the door before opening it. The hallway was silent. Maybe I could clear off before Edward noticed. I walked to the stairs on tiptoe, trying to be as quiet as possible. I heard someone clearing his throat, which stopped me in my tracks. I froze. Edward was standing behind me. I took a deep breath before turning around to face at him. He looked me up and down with an inscrutable expression. I realized I was wearing nothing but his shirt. I started pulling it down to try to cover my legs.

"Your clothes are in the bathroom. They should be dry."

"Where's the bathroom?"

"Second door at the end of the hallway; don't go into the room next to it."

He rushed down the stairs before I had a chance to say anything at all. He had aroused my curiosity by forbidding me to go into one of the rooms. But I wasn't about to tempt fate. I went to find my clothes. This is a real bachelor's bathroom, I thought as I went inside. Towels rolled up in a ball, some shower gel, a toothbrush, and a mirror in which you could hardly see a thing. My clothes were hanging on a heated towel rail and were dry. I took off the shirt and felt greatly relived. I held it without knowing exactly what to do with it. I spotted a basket with dirty clothes. It was bad enough I'd slept in his bed; I didn't need to see his dirty boxer shorts from the day before. I found a clothes hanger, perfect. I automatically splashed water on my face, which felt wonderful; I had the impression that I was thinking more clearly. I used the sleeve of my sweatshirt to dry myself. I was ready to face Edward, and perhaps to answer his questions.

I stood at the entrance to his living room, rocking back and forth. Postman Pat trotted in and rubbed against my legs. I petted him to avoid talking to his master, who had his back to me behind the kitchen counter.

"Coffee?" he asked suddenly.

"Yes," I replied, walking toward him.

"Are you hungry?"

"I'll eat later; the coffee will be enough."

He put some food on a plate and set it down on the counter. The smell of the scrambled eggs made my mouth water. I looked at the plate defiantly.

"Sit down and eat."

I automatically obeyed him, partly because I was starving and partly because his tone of voice left me no choice. Edward was standing and staring at me, holding his coffee, with a cigarette hanging out of his mouth. I brought the fork to my lips and opened my eyes wide. He may not have been very friendly but his scrambled eggs were worthy of a cordon bleu chef. Every now and again, I looked up from my plate. Impossible to work out what he was thinking or to bear the way he was staring at me for long.

I started looking around. One fact stood out: Edward's place was a complete shambles. There were things everywhere: photography material, magazines, books, piles of clothes, half-full ashtrays. A pack of cigarettes hit my cup; I turned and looked at my host.

"You're dying for one," he said.

"Thanks."

I got off my stool, took my dose of nicotine, and walked over to the bay window.

"Edward, I have to explain what happened yesterday."

"Not at all; I would have helped anyone."

"Contrary to what you think, I'm not in the habit of making a spectacle of myself like that. I want you to understand."

"I don't care what made you do it."

He walked over to the front door and opened it. This oaf was telling me to leave. His dog was still nestled against me; I petted him one last time. Then I walked past his master and stood on the steps. I turned to face him and looked him straight in the eyes. No one could be so hard.

"Goodbye," he said.

"If you need anything," I said, "please don't hesitate."

"I don't need anything."

He slammed the door in my face. I stood there for several minutes. What an asshole this guy was.

I had to do a big spring clean to get my house back in order. When it came to getting plastered and having a hangover, it didn't matter what country you were in: the effects were the same.

Felix had played his role as a counselor wonderfully, listening to me for many hours at a time over the phone. I'd just gone through another crisis and I was still standing. I was going to launch into a new attempt to get better.

I was trying to find a way to go about it when someone knocked on my door. I was surprised to find my neighbor there. The gods were against me. I hadn't seen him since I'd left his place, a week before, and I was none the worse for it.

"Hello," he said dryly.

"Edward."

"Actually, I do have a favor to ask you. Can you take care of my dog?"

"Don't Abby and Jack usually take care of him?"

"I'm going to be away too long to leave him with them."

"What do you mean by too long?"

"Two weeks or more."

"When do you want me to take him?"

"Now."

He certainly had nerve. And he'd left his motor running, so he was really holding a gun to my head.

Since I was taking my time to answer, he shook his head and said, "OK. Forget it."

"Do you mind if I think about it for a second?"

"Think about watching a dog?"

"Well, since you've asked so nicely . . . Fine, bring him in."

He went and opened the back of his Land Rover and Postman Pat jumped out. More affectionate than his master, he was delighted to see me, which made me smile.

"I'm off," said Edward.

He sat down behind the wheel.

"Wait a minute, doesn't he have a leash?"

"No, you whistle and he comes back."

"That's it?"

Edward closed the car door and sped off. Still the same jerk. And he'd taken up the nasty habit of slamming every single door in my face.

Three weeks had passed since I'd become a dog sitter. Three weeks. Edward was really going too far. But the dog was sweet; my best friend for the moment. My only friend in this hellhole, in fact. He followed me everywhere, even slept with me. I frightened myself a little when I started talking to him. It was a bit like, "Who's mommy's good little boy, then?" But even when he was being a good doggie, he still looked more like a donkey crossed with a bear. A mixture you couldn't actually define.

I discovered the joys of having a four-legged friend. I liked it, except when he ran off. I was treated to at least one of his escapades every day when we walked along the beach. Even though I wore myself out whistling for him, nothing happened. Today, I was worried even more than usual. He'd been gone too long.

I was soaked in sweat from running down the beach, coughing my brains out. Head down, hands on my knees, I was catching my breath when I heard Postman Pat barking. He was coming toward me accompanied by a woman I'd never seen before. I shaded my eyes with my hand. The closer she got, the more I knew I wouldn't have run across this young woman without noticing her. She must have been about my age. She was wearing a short kilt and walking boots. She looked like she was about to catch pneumonia: under her leather vest, her top was very low-cut and barely covered her breasts. She had a mass of curly auburn hair. Before she got to me, she picked up a stick and threw it far away for the dog.

"Get lost, you dirty beast," she said, laughing.

She kept smiling as she continued walking towards me.

"Hi, Diane," she said, before giving me a hug.

"Hello," I replied, taken aback.

"I found out you were taking care of him and I came to see if he wasn't giving you too much of a hard time."

"No, I'm doing fine, except for now."

"Oh, don't worry; I can't count the number of times I wound up with my ass in the sand running after him. He only listens to Edward. Though who would dare try anything else with my brother?"

She burst out laughing, but she talked so incredibly fast I wasn't sure I'd understood everything.

"Edward's your brother?"

"Yes. Oh, sorry, I haven't introduced myself: I'm Judith, his younger sister."

"And I'm Diane, but you know that already."

"Good, so now you'll offer me something to drink at your place?"

She linked arms with me, turned us around and headed towards the cottage. This young woman wasn't Edward's sister; their parents couldn't possibly have given birth to two such different children. The only thing they had in common was the color of their eyes; Judith's were exactly the same greenish-blue as Edward's.

I showed her in and she immediately collapsed on the sofa and put her feet on the coffee table.

"Would you like coffee, tea?"

"You're French, right, so you must have a good bottle of wine. It's time for a drink."

Five minutes later, we were clinking glasses.

"Diane, I can't believe you're as antisocial as my brother. Why are you living here? It's a beautiful place, that's true, but what were you thinking?"

"It's an experience like any other, living all alone by the sea. But what about you? Where do you live?"

"Above a pub in Dublin. You have to come."

"Maybe one day."

"How long are you here for? Aren't you working?"

"Not for the moment. And you?"

"I'm having a few days off, but I'm doing some work at the port. I'm managing the schedules for the containers; it's not very exciting but it pays the rent and bills."

She continued jabbering, a real chatterbox. Then she suddenly shot up, as if she'd been stung by a bee.

"I'm off; Abby and Jack are expecting me."

She was already on her way out the door.

"Wait, you've left your ciggies."

"Keep them; they're contraband. I have a little arrangement with the dockers," she said, winking at me.

"You're walking home? It's dark out. Do you want me to drive you back?"

"Are you kidding? It'll be some exercise for my thighs. See you tomorrow!"

Judith came back the next day as she said. Then the day after. Three days in a row she'd invaded my personal space. Yet, paradoxically, her presence didn't suffocate me. She made me laugh. She was a born flirt. She knew how to show off her figure— she could have been an Italian actress—and swore like a trooper every time she opened her mouth. Dynamite. She bombarded me with cock-and-bull stories about her love life. Even though she was very confident and didn't fear a thing, any good-looking guy who came along could take advantage of her. She couldn't resist any bad boy who tried to pick her up.

That night, she stayed to have dinner with me. She ate enough for four people and could hold her liquor like a man.

"It's just us," she said, unbuttoning her jeans, "Do you mind?"

I went and opened the door for the dog who was asking for his nighttime walk.

"Why did my brother leave you his mutt?"

"I owed him a favor."

She looked at me suspiciously. Without reacting, I sat down on the couch and tucked my legs underneath me.

"Has Edward always been like he is?"

"What do you mean by 'like he is'?" she answered, using air quotes.

"Kind of angry, unsociable, taciturn . . ."

"Oh, that? Yes, always. He's had a fucking awful character since he was born."

"Nice. I feel sorry for your parents."

"Didn't Abby tell you anything? They were the ones who brought us up—Abby and Jack. Our mother died giving birth to me; Edward was six years old. Our father didn't want to take care of us, so he sent us to our aunt and uncle."

"I'm really sorry . . ."

"Don't be. I had wonderful parents and wanted for nothing. You'll never hear me call myself an orphan."

"You never lived with your father?"

"We did spend a few days with him, when he deigned to come out of his office, but it was hellish. Because of Edward."

"Edward wasn't happy to see him?"

"No. He thinks our parents abandoned us. He holds a grudge against the whole world. In spite of all the admiration he had for Dad, as soon as they were in the same room, they'd start fighting."

"What do you mean?"

"Edward is exactly like him. So there have always been sparks between them. They spent all their time shouting at each other."

"What about you? Were you caught in the middle?"

"Yes. You can imagine the atmosphere."

"And are things as confrontational as ever?"

"Dad died."

"Oh . . ."

"Yeah, we've had some hard times."

She gave a little laugh, lit a cigarette, and stared out into space for a few seconds before continuing.

"They fought right up to the end, but Edward stayed with Dad throughout his whole illness. He spent hours at his bedside. I think they made their peace. I never found out what they said to each other. Edward won't talk about it; he just assured me that Dad died peacefully."

"How old were you?"

"I was sixteen and Edward was twenty-two. He

immediately decreed that he was now head of the family and had to provide for me. Abby and Jack couldn't do anything about it. He came and got me and took me to live with him."

"How did he manage everything?"

"No idea. He was going to college, working, and taking care of me. As he got older, he created a shell around him to protect himself from everything and everyone."

"Doesn't he have any friends?"

"A few, hand-picked. It's almost impossible for him to trust anyone. He's convinced he'll either be betrayed or abandoned. He taught me to get along by myself and not to count on anyone. He always protected me and never hesitated to get into a fight to defend me from guys he thought were coming on to me too much."

"Is he violent?"

"Not really; he fights when people really annoy him, you know, when he gets pushed too far."

"I think that's exactly what I did," I mumbled.

She looked at me, screwing up her eyes.

"You're not afraid of him though, are you?"

"I don't know. He was really nasty to me."

She burst out laughing.

"Well, you coming here must have really pissed him off, but don't worry: he has high principles. Amongst them, never to raise a hand to a woman. He'd more likely be the kind of guy to help a damsel in distress."

"I'm having trouble imagining that the person you're describing is my neighbor."

Judith was going back to Dublin the next day. She met me on my daily walk along the beach with Postman Pat. We were sitting on the sand. She was trying to find out some information about me again.

"You're hiding something. What are you doing here? I can't believe that neither Abby or I have been able to worm anything out of you."

"There's nothing to tell. My life isn't interesting, I can assure you."

I left to find Postman Pat. He'd taken off out of sight again. I ran towards the path that led to the cottages. I was always afraid that he'd get hit by a car, or worse, that Edward would come back to find his dog wandering around.

I caught him and pulled him by the collar to take him back to the beach. At that very moment, Edward's Land Rover pulled up in front of the cottages. To prove I could really control the dog, I held on to him firmly until his master was standing next to us. He was jumping all over Edward, who was looking daggers at me. We stood there staring at each other while the dog ran back and forth between us.

A high-pitched scream rang out. Judith ran over to us. She leaped onto her brother. I thought I could see the glimpse of a smile on Edward's face. She finally let him go. She took hold of his chin and stared at him, frowning.

"You don't look so good."

"Stop that."

He broke free and turned toward me.

"Thanks for the dog."

"You're welcome."

Judith started applauding, looking back and forth at each of us.

"Hell! What a conversation! Edward, you put more than two words together. And you, Diane, you're more chatty than usual."

I shrugged my shoulders.

"Judith, that's enough," Edward groaned.

"Oh, stop your moaning!"

"Abby and Jack are waiting for us."

"Let me say goodbye to my new friend."

Edward raised his eyes to heaven and went on ahead. Judith wrapped her arms around me.

"I'm coming back in two weeks for Christmas vacation. I'll come and see you and you'll confess all."

"I don't think so."

I hugged her back; being with this young woman did me good.

I stayed on the beach and watched them leave. Judith was prancing about next to her brother, happy to be with him. And he seemed happy too, in his own way.

5

I hadn't heard from Felix in over a week. That was
the last straw; now I was the one who wanted to get
hold of him. After three tries, he finally answered
the phone.

"Diane, I've got too much to do!"

"Hello to you, too!"

"Talk fast; I've got so many things to get ready
for Christmas."

"What are you planning?"

"Your parents told me you weren't coming home
for Christmas. They invited me over but I said no.

They'd try to exorcise me again. Instead, it's going to be a beach party in Mykonos."

"Really? OK."

"I'll call you when I get back."

He hung up. I stood for a few moments with the phone against my ear. It just gets better and better. Out of sight, out of mind. The fact that my parents didn't try to convince me to come home for the holidays was hardly surprising. Their depressed, widowed daughter would have spoiled their sociable dinner. But Felix dropping me, that was a harder pill to swallow.

Bright winter sunshine filled the living room— like I'd never seen before—and yet, I didn't have the energy to go out. The approaching Christmas merriment filled me with gloomy thoughts. Someone knocking on my door forced me out of my armchair. I went to answer it. Judith was dressed like one of Santa's little helpers, the sexy version. She threw her arms around my neck.

"What are you doing locked away indoors in such gorgeous weather? Get your gloves on and we'll go for a walk."

"You're kind, but no thanks."

"You think I'm giving you a choice," she said, pushing me towards the coat closet.

She pulled a hat down on my head, picked up my keys and locked the cottage door.

She sang all the Christmas songs—out of tune. I laughed, in spite of myself. Judith produced a miracle of sorts. She got me to walk along the entire bay and through Mulranny to drag me over to Abby and Jack's place.

"We're here!" she shouted as we went inside.

I followed her into the living room. She went and planted big, wet kisses on her aunt and uncle's cheeks.

"Diane, so good to see you," Abby said, giving me a big hug.

Jack gave me a broad smile and a gentle tap on the shoulder. All we needed was stories by Dickens to re-create the myth of Christmas. The tree was as high as the ceiling, cards lined up on the mantelpiece, gingerbread cookies on the coffee table, brightly lit garlands, a remix of "Jingle Bells" in the background: it was all there. Within minutes,

Judith and Abby were making me feel at home. They forced me to sit down; Judith handed me a cup of tea and Abby a plate of cookies, carrot cake, and gingerbread. You'd think they were trying to fatten me up. Jack threw his head back and laughed.

For two hours, it was like watching a play. Judith sat on the floor and wrapped presents that she threw under the tree. Abby was knitting a Christmas stocking. I was completely at odds with this atmosphere that reeked of good spirits. I didn't believe in any of it any more. Yet, in the past, I would have been the first to put on a party hat and throw confetti. All for Clara.

"Be careful," Jack said to me, "they're plotting and I think it's something to do with you."

"Be quiet," Abby said. "Diane, Christmas is in two days. You're not going back to France?"

"No, I'm not."

The fake smile I'd worn since I arrived was gradually fading.

"Well then, come and spend it with us. We're staying home, just us."

Just us? Was that bastard Edward going to be coming, too? The mere idea of seeing him be the life of the party on Christmas Eve was enough to tempt me to accept.

"Come on," Judith begged. "I don't want you to be all by yourself."

I was about to reply when we heard a door bang shut. Judith got up and skipped out to the entrance hall. We could hear the sound of a muted conversation.

"Come on, now," said Judith, "and behave yourself!"

I wasn't surprised to see Edward appear behind his sister. Instead of sitting down again, Judith put her arm around his neck, leaned her chin against his shoulder, smiled, and looked at me.

"Say hello, Edward!" she shouted, still staring at me.

To stop myself from bursting out laughing, I looked up at him. The best way to annoy him. He gave me a hard look.

"Hello," he muttered.

"Edward."

He came into the room, shook Jack's hand and stood in front of the fireplace. He turned his back on us and watched the fire.

"Now everyone's said hello," said Judith, "let's get back to our discussion."

"We're serious," continued Abby. "Come and celebrate Christmas with us."

Edward quickly turned around.

"What are you talking about? This isn't the Salvation Army."

His whole body had gone rigid and I wouldn't have been surprised to see smoke come out of his ears.

"Don't you ever get sick of being an ass?" his sister retorted. "We've invited Diane to spend Christmas, and you have nothing to say about it. If you don't like it, you can stay home; we can live without you."

The brother and sister were at each other's throats; they looked like two cocks in a fight. But for once, Edward didn't seem the more dangerous one. In spite of the pleasure it gave me to see him get thrashed by his younger sister, I had to put an end to it.

"Just a minute! I think that I might have something to say about this. I won't be coming because I don't celebrate Christmas."

"But . . ."

"Don't insist."

"You do what you like," Jack said. "But if you change your mind, our door is always open to you."

"Thanks very much. I'll be going now; it's getting late."

"Stay for dinner," Abby offered.

"No, thank you anyway. Don't get up; I know the way out."

Judith stood back. Abby hugged me again. I could see the disapproving look she shot at her nephew. I went and gave Jack a kiss on the cheek. He winked at me. I went over to Edward and stood in front of him. He looked me straight in the eyes.

"Thanks," I whispered, so no one else could hear me. "You've just done me a big favor. You're not so bad after all."

"Get the hell out of here," he mumbled between clenched teeth.

"Goodbye," I said, loudly.

He didn't reply. I gave a last little wave and found Judith near the front door. She watched me put on my coat.

"Why are you running away?"

"I want to go back home."

"I'll come and see you over Christmas."

"No. I want to be alone. Your place is with your family."

"Is it because of my idiot brother?"

"He doesn't matter to me at all. It's got nothing to do with him. I have to go. Good night. Don't worry about me," I said, giving her a hug and a kiss.

I'd forgotten I had walked all the way there. Rain was beating down on me and it was dark. I pushed my hands deep into my pockets and kept walking, trying not to think. The sound of a car honking made me jump. I stopped and turned around, but the headlights were blinding me. I was even more surprised to see Edward's car stop next to me. He opened the window.

"Get in."

"Is this the spirit of Christmas? Or are you not feeling well?"

"Take advantage of the offer of a ride; it won't happen again."

"I suppose you have to be good for something."

I got into the car. His car was as messy as his house. I had to kick things away on the floor in order to sit down. The dashboard was full of packs of cigarettes and newspapers, and old coffee cups were stuffed into the sides of the doors. God knows I'm a smoker, but the smell of the cold tobacco made me feel sick. Nothing but silence in the driver's seat.

"Why haven't you gone back to France?"

"I don't feel like it's home any more," I replied, a little too quickly.

"But you're not at home here, either."

"Wait a minute. Is that why you offered to drive me back? So you could insult me some more?"

"The only thing I care about where you're concerned is when you're leaving."

"Stop your damned car!"

He stopped short. I wanted to get out as quickly as possible, but I couldn't unbuckle my seatbelt.

"Need some help?"

"Shut up," I shouted.

I finally managed to free myself, and for once, I was the one slamming the door in his face. Well, the car door, at least.

"Merry Christmas!" he called out from the window.

I didn't even look at him, just started walking. His car passed near me, went through a puddle and soaked me from head to foot. He had a mental age of twelve, if that. He would end up winning; as well as getting on my nerves, he was wearing me out.

I finally got home, shivering, and barricaded myself in.

It was December 26, eleven o'clock in the morning and someone was knocking at my door. Judith. She pushed me aside and came in.

"Christmas is over!"

She went into the kitchen to get herself a coffee and came back to crash down on the couch.

"There's really something not right with you," she said. "I have a favor to ask."

"I'm listening."

"Every year, I organize the New Year's Eve party."

I could feel myself turning white. I stood up and lit a cigarette.

"The owner of the pub knows me since I was a little girl; he can't refuse me anything. You know that only old people live in Mulranny, and dancing isn't really their thing. So I borrow the pub and do what I like. We've had some wild times there."

"I can imagine."

"Every year, all my friends come and we have a great time. We booze it up, sing, dance on the tables . . . And this year, we'll have a French woman with us."

"Oh? Are there two of us in Mulranny?"

"Stop it, Diane. You don't celebrate Christmas, fine. You're not the only one who has a problem with family gatherings. But New Year's Eve, that's the time to be with friends, to have fun; you can't refuse."

"You're asking too much of me."

"Why?"

"Drop it."

"OK. I want you to be there, but try to avoid the junkshop."

I frowned.

"Forget the yoga pants and the awful sweatshirt."

In a different way, she was becoming as annoying as her brother. I sighed and closed my eyes before replying.

"Fine, I'll come, but I won't stay for long."

"That's what you think. Good, that's settled; I've got a lot on my plate."

She swept out like a tornado. I slumped down into my armchair and held my head in my hands.

I managed to convince Judith that I could do without her fashion advice. I still knew how to dress by myself and I imagined that her tips would have been in the worst possible taste.

I considered my reflection in the swing mirror. I felt like I was in disguise, and yet, I was rediscovering myself. I looked at myself for a long time in the mirror. There was no doubt about it: I had aged, my face showed the signs. Wrinkles had appeared, and when I looked closer, I could see some grey hairs. And then I thought of Colin. So I hid some of the traces of my sadness with makeup. I darkened my eyelids and put a thick coat of mascara on my eyelashes; I made my eyes stand out for him. I instinctively tied my hair up in a messy bun; a few strands of hair fell down onto my neck. He always used to play with them. I dressed in black from head to foot, pants, a top that was open at the back and high heels. My only piece of jewelry was my wedding ring that was hidden between my breasts.

I was in front of the pub. The parking lot was full and the party in full swing. I was about to find myself in the midst of a bunch of complete strangers. I was going to have to talk and smile; I didn't think I could do it.

I took a deep breath and opened the door. The heat took me by surprise. The place was jam-packed with everyone singing, dancing, and laughing to the sound of "Sweet Home Alabama". There was no doubt about it: the Irish certainly knew how to party. I'd never seen anything like it. I had no trouble finding Judith. You couldn't help but spot her lion's mane, black leather pants, and red bustier. I managed to make my way over to her. I tapped her lightly on the shoulder and she turned around.

"Is that you, Diane?" she asked, looking puzzled.

"Yes, you idiot!"

"I was sure there was a femme fatale hiding somewhere in you. Shit, you're going to steal the show from me!"

"Stop or I'll go."

"No way. You're here and you're staying."

"I warned you: as soon as it's midnight, I'll be like Cinderella and disappear."

She went away for a few minutes, then came back and handed me a glass.

"Have a drink and we'll talk about it later!"

She whisked me around, introducing me to everyone. I met some really nice people; they were all smiling and wanting to have a good time in a way I'd never imagined possible. The atmosphere was all friendly, not at all full of show-offs. The many glasses of wine I was given during the evening helped me to relax and join in the fun.

I kept on smiling and managed to make it to the bar. My glass had been empty far too long, and if I wanted to see in the New Year, I had no choice but to keep drinking. So I didn't skimp on the alcohol. I could sense someone next to me but didn't think anything of it; I just continued stirring my cocktail. If my level of rum was already high, my friend at the bar had drunk enough whisky to cause a tsunami. I knew his hands; I'd already seen them. Annoyed, I looked up. Edward was leaning on the bar, sipping his drink and watching me. I had the impression I was going through a metal detector.

"My sister's done it again," he said, smirking. "She's always been fascinated by stray dogs."

"And what about you? How many people are you going to attack tonight?"

"Just you, no one else. They're my friends."

"Who'd want to be friends with you?"

I turned and walked away. The evening looked as though it might get more difficult.

I half-listened to people's conversations. Judith was standing next to me; she wouldn't let me out of her sight in case I ran off. I was distracted by the sight of a tanned, bald head. I pushed everyone aside to get to him.

"Felix!"

He turned around and spotted me. He ran towards me. I threw myself in his arms and he swung me around. I was laughing and crying, my face in the crook of his neck. He was crushing me, but Felix hugging me so hard that I'd get black and blue marks was worth it.

"When I got your message, I couldn't resist."

"I've missed you so much! Thank you."

He put me down and held my face in his hands.

"I told you you couldn't live without me!"

I gave him a little slap on the back of the head. He held me tight again.

"It's really good to see you."

"How long are you staying?"

"I'm going back tomorrow night."

I put my arms around his waist and squeezed him tight.

"Where do you get a drink in your pub?"

I took his hand and led him to the counter. He drank his first drink all at once and got himself another. He assumed he had some catching up to do. He didn't forget to fill my glass up, either.

"You've gotten stronger. You look great when you make an effort."

"I'm playing the game for tonight, and for Judith."

"Point her out to me."

"No need to find me, I'm right here."

I turned towards her, smiling.

"You should have told me that your man would be coming tonight," she said, sulking.

"My what?"

"Umm, your man, your guy . . ."

"Stop! It's just Felix . . ."

"Thanks for the 'just'," he said, cutting in.

"That's enough from you. Judith, I'd like you to meet my best friend."

She gave me a hard stare, thrust her ample bosom forward and stood on tiptoe to give Felix a peck on the cheek.

"Diane was right to invite you," she said. "I like a bit of warm new flesh, I like it a lot . . . an awful lot."

She tilted her head to one side and studied him from all angles. He fulfilled all the criteria of someone she'd fall for: shaved head, leather shirt, T-shirt with such a low-cut V that you could almost see his belly-button.

"I'm very pleased to meet you," he said, giving her his most charming smile.

"And so am I. I hope that Diane is willing to share."

I gave a discreet little kick to my seductive, narcissistic best friend.

"Don't worry. We have all night to get to know each other better, but there's something I have to tell you."

"I'm all ears," she replied, batting her eyelashes.

"It will never work between us."

"Oh! I've never been told to get lost so fast. Does my breath smell? Have I got something between my teeth?"

"No. You just *don't* have something between your legs."

I raised my eyes to heaven. Judith burst out laughing.

"OK. At least help me keep her here until dawn," she said, nodding towards me.

"I know exactly how to do that."

He handed me a Jell-O shot. My throat was burning but I couldn't care less. I knew that between the two of them, I wouldn't be able to resist for long.

Midnight came around quickly. All the guests counted down the twelve rings, except for me and Felix. We were standing to one side, holding hands. When everyone started shouting, I leaned my head against his shoulder.

"Happy New Year, Diane."

"You, too. Come on, let's find Judith."

I led him along behind me. I quickly found who we were looking for.

"Why are you stopping?" Felix asked, bumping into me.

"She's with her damned brother."

"He's quite a good-looking guy."

"He's horrible! You don't know who you're talking about. He's my neighbor."

"You should have told me that the scenery was so attractive, I would have come sooner."

"Don't talk nonsense. Too bad, we'll see her later."

"I'll take my chances, if you don't mind."

I turned quickly to face him. Felix's lustful look said it all. He found Edward to his taste.

"You are really sick!"

"Not at all. Think about it. I could tame the

beast and whisper in his ear that he should be nice to you."

"Stop talking nonsense. Ask me to dance instead."

I moved from one wild rock song to the next with Felix, and danced up a frenzy with Judith. We sang along enthusiastically to hits from the Irish gods, U2. Every one of the guests went into a kind of trance when Bono's voice echoed through the pub. I quenched my thirst in between dances with large cocktails. Every now and then, I went outside to the back terrace to get some air.

Smoking a cigarette and holding a drink, I looked through the window and watched Judith and Felix. He was giving her a very private lesson on how to dance the Bachata to the off-beat rock rhythm of the Kings of Leon and their "Sex on Fire". Hilarious. Edward charged over and stood in front of me.

"Can't I even have a cigarette in peace?" I said.

"Go tell your show-off friend to leave my sister the hell alone."

"She doesn't look like she's complaining."

"Get him away from her or I'll deal with him."

I stood up to my full height and walked closer to him. I poked him in the chest, which was meant to be as threatening as his words.

"Your sister doesn't need you to protect her. And you're the one who should watch out for Felix. You might find that he really likes you, and he's managed to sleep with guys much straighter than you."

He grabbed my wrist and pushed me angrily against the railing. His eyes pierced mine. He pulled me tight against him and squeezed my wrist harder.

"Don't push me too far!"

"Or what? You'll hit me?"

"I'm thinking about it."

"Let go of me—now."

I took a last drag on my cigarette, blew the smoke out in his face, and dropped the butt at his feet. It was only when I got inside that I realized my legs were shaking.

"Well, then," Felix said, coming over to me, "so things heated up between you and your neighbor."

"I tried to fix things up for you."

I ditched him to get a refill; I needed a drink.

The time passed. There was as much alcohol in people's bodies as there was on the floor. Both the air and everyone's skin were damp and smelled slightly of sweat. I danced so much that I couldn't feel my feet any more. I was really having a good time; I was light-headed and couldn't believe it. Except that my advanced state of drunkenness was starting to make me dizzy. I couldn't walk straight any more, I couldn't see very well, I was laughing too loudly, and I was losing my inhibitions. The proof was my very personal rendition of "I Love Rock 'n' Roll"; I'd never have Joan Jett's talent. I walked off the dance floor to join Judith and Felix who were filling up their glasses at the bar.

"I'm going home. I've had it."

"I'll have one last drink and then see you at your place," Felix said.

"Are you sure you want to go home to bed?" asked Judith.

"Yes, the show is over! Thank you for tonight; I didn't think I was still capable of having a good time," I replied, giving her a big hug.

I was rummaging through my bag looking for

my keys while walking towards the exit. I bumped into someone.

"Sorry."

"Always in my way!" Edward replied.

"Get lost, I'm going home."

I pushed him aside and got out into the fresh air. Even though there was a biting wind, it didn't help sober me up.

I was driving slowly towards my cottage. At least some of my reflexes were still working. I had to admit that I was creeping along, clutching the steering wheel—another little old lady's habit. I was startled by a car that was tailgating me. The driver flashed his headlights. I willingly slowed down. He reacted immediately, pulling out ahead and cutting me off. I recognized Edward's car. He wanted war, well, he'd have it.

When I got to my place, I put on the hand brake and ran over to his house.

"Open this door right now!" I shouted, banging on it. "Get out here at once!"

I started pacing back and forth while continuing to shout. I'd had enough; I picked up some stones from the ground and sent them flying at his door and windows.

"You're completely nuts!" he shouted when he finally came outside.

"You're the one who's sick. You're nothing but a reckless driver and a total shit! We're going to sort things out between us once and for all."

"Go sleep it off somewhere."

"I'm worse than a leech: the more you tell me to go away, the longer I'll stay."

"I should have let you rot on the beach." He stood in his doorway, his arms crossed.

"You have no idea what you're talking about," I screamed, hitting him. "You know nothing at all."

I was hammering him with all my strength, trying to scratch him. He defended himself against my attack half-heartedly just using his arms.

"Calm down!" I heard Felix say behind me.

He put his arm around my waist, lifted me up and pulled me away from Edward. I continued hitting into thin air.

"Let go of me; I'm going to tear him apart."

"It's not worth it," he replied, tightening his grip on me.

I started kicking, trying to give Edward a good bash with my high heels.

"Watch out for your family jewels, asshole," I shouted.

"Lock her up," Edward roared. "She's completely mad."

"Shut it!" Felix shouted, whirling us back to face him.

Felix's reply made me stop moving. As for Edward, he looked disconcerted and stared wide-eyed at Felix.

"You're as crazy as each other," he muttered, turning to go inside.

"Stay where you are," Felix said. "We're not done yet."

He put me down and cupped my face in his hands.

"You're going to promise me that you'll go home and stay there, all right?"

"No."

"Let me deal with this. Go home to bed and get some sleep. I'll see you tomorrow. Trust me, it will be fine."

He kissed me on the forehead and pushed me away.

I was staggering more than walking, turning around to see what was going on every two steps. Felix and Edward were still in the same spot; I couldn't hear what they were fighting about.

Once I got home, I dragged myself upstairs and slid under the covers. In spite of being worried about Felix, I was exhausted. The stress, alcohol, and tiredness wore me down completely.

6

Moving in my bed made my head ache. With great difficulty, I tried to open my eyes, but they stung. My tongue was furry and I ached all over. Even before trying to stand up, I knew that the day would feel interminable. That would teach me to play the fool at a party. I opened the curtains to try to wake myself up. Who owned that car parked in front of my house? I had the feeling that I was missing something enormously important about the night before. My first shot of caffeine of the day would help me fill in the blanks. Going downstairs was painful, that's how much my head throbbed. There was a body stretched out on my couch. The fog began to lift.

Felix. One of his arms and legs were hanging down onto the floor. He was still dressed and snoring like an engine. I couldn't see his face.

"Wake up," I said, shaking him.

"Be quiet; I want to sleep."

"How are you? Are you all right?"

"I feel like I've been hit by a bulldozer."

He sat up, still with his head down and rubbed the back of his neck.

"Felix, look at me."

He raised his head. He had a cut on one eyebrow and a bad black eye. He sank back on the couch, holding his sides and grimacing in pain. I went over to him and lifted up his T-shirt; he had an enormous bruise.

"Good God, what did he do to you?"

Felix leaped off the couch and charged at the mirror.

"It's OK. I'm still good-looking."

He touched his face, flexed his muscles, and smiled at himself.

"I'll still be able to show off when I get back to Paris."

"There's nothing funny about all this; he's dangerous. You were lucky."

He swept away my comments with a brush of the hand and went back to collapse on the couch, but not without wincing in pain. The fool hurt everywhere.

"That said, the next time you go into exile, go to the land of the Pygmies! Shit, no doubt about it, that guy is Irish. He must have learned how to walk on a rugby pitch. When he knocked me to the ground I thought I was playing in the Six Nations tournament . . ."

"So to sum it up, you got your kicks fighting with that jerk."

"I swear, I was on the pitch and the crowd was going wild."

"And you were the rugby ball. That's all very well, but did you manage to get a punch in?"

"I hesitated. I didn't want to smash up his pretty face."

"You're making fun of me!"

"Yes and no. But you can be sure of one thing: I defended your honor. I gave him a good left hook; he's in no shape to French kiss anyone."

"Really?"

"Blood spurted out all over the place and his lip blew up to twice its size. Give me five!"

I did a little victory dance. In the shower, I was still laughing about Felix's exploits. He didn't stop talking all through breakfast. He gave me all the news from Paris and told me how our apartment had been cleared out. My parents and Colin's had taken everything; nothing was left. Then he told me about the accounts for the book café. There were almost no sales any more. One day or other, I was going to have to take things in hand.

Wrapped in my bath towel, I thought about my lack of desire to return to France. I caught sight of myself in the mirror and got upset. There was nothing around my neck.

"Felix!"

"What?" he shouted, coming up the stairs four at a time.

"I've lost my wedding ring."

I started sobbing.

"What did you say?"

"I was wearing it around my neck yesterday."

"Don't worry, we'll find it. You must have lost it at the pub; get dressed."

Ten minutes later we were on the road. The pub was closed; I told Felix how to get to Abby and Jack's. Judith would have the key. I went and knocked on the door while Felix searched through the car.

"What a surprise to see you today," said Abby, opening the door.

"Hello, Abby. I'd like to see Judith, it's urgent."

"She's sleeping, but maybe I could help?"

"I have to get into the pub. I lost something last night," I explained, tears in my eyes.

"What's the matter, my darling?"

"Please, help me."

Felix was holding me in his arms when Abby, Jack, and Judith met us at the pub. Judith rushed over to us, but focused on Felix.

"What happened?" she asked, touching his eye. "Jack, take care of him."

"It's nothing; I had a little romp with your brother."

"You did what with my brother?"

"*Secret boy*, that's all I can say. Let's just say there were a lot of muscles involved. But that doesn't matter. Take care of Diane."

"If you say so. Right. Your turn now," she said, opening the door for me. "It had better be important because I want to know what's going on."

"It is."

I went inside the pub and stood petrified for a few minutes.

"You've already cleaned up?"

"Yes, they're open tonight. I had just gone to sleep when Abby dragged me out of bed. So what exactly did you lose?"

"A piece of jewelry."

I started looking around on the floor.

"No one died; you'll buy yourself another one."

"No," I said loudly, and I suddenly stood up. Judith took a step backwards.

"It's not Judith's fault," Felix said, coming over to me. "Come on, we'll both look."

We each went to opposite ends of the pub. I crawled along the floor, feeling along the cracks in the parquet in the hopes I would find the chain.

"Diane," Abby said softly, kneeling down beside me. "Diane, look at me."

She put her hand on my arm.

"I don't have time."

"Tell us what you're looking for; we can help you."

"I lost my wedding ring. I wear it around my neck."

"You're married?" asked Judith.

I couldn't say a word.

"Let's leave Diane to look by herself," said Abby.

I withdrew into my shell, hearing nothing of anything that was happening around me. I crept forward on my hands and knees, pushing the tables and bar stools out of the way, scratching in the cracks between the floorboards to see if the chain hadn't slipped down.

"Where are the garbage cans?" I asked, standing up.

"I've already looked, there's nothing," Felix replied.

"You didn't look hard enough."

I sank to the ground, holding my stomach and sobbing. Felix took me in his arms and rocked me. I beat his chest with my fists.

"Calm down . . . calm down . . ."

"It's not possible; I can't have lost it."

"I'm so sorry."

"Maybe it's time to turn the page," Judith suggested. "I don't know, but if your husband dumped you . . ."

"He didn't 'dump' me."

Felix took my hand and squeezed it tight. I tried to breathe and crushed myself against him again. Without letting go of him, I turned towards Judith.

"Colin is . . . Colin is dead."

"Tell her everything," Felix whispered in my ear.

"And Clara . . . our daughter . . . died with him."

Judith gasped and covered her mouth with her hand. Felix helped me stand up. I looked over at Jack and Abby without really seeing them.

"I'm going to keep looking; I'll find it. I promise," said Judith.

Abby and Jack just hugged me tight while I stood there, my arms dangling at my sides and staring into space. Felix supported me and got me in the car. He fastened my seat belt and headed for the cottage.

He helped me into bed. After making me take some aspirin, he stretched out beside me and took me in his arms. I lost all sense of time. All I felt was emptiness.

"I have to go," Felix said. "I have to catch my plane. Do you want to come back with me?"

"No, I'm staying here."

"I'll call you very soon."

I turned my back on him. He gave me a kiss. I didn't respond. I could hear his footsteps. He silently closed the front door. I heard his car moving away. I was alone. And Colin and Clara had died a second time.

For three days, I'd sat prostrate in an armchair in the living room. I kept pictures of Colin and Clara in my hands. Before going back to Dublin, Judith had come to say goodbye. She hadn't found my wedding ring.

When someone else started knocking at my door, I dragged my feet while going to answer it. Edward was standing there.

"You're the last person I want to see," I said, starting to shut the door.

"Wait," he replied, keeping it open with his fist.

"What do you want?"

"To give you this; I just found it in front of my house. It must have fallen off the other night. Here."

I couldn't even move. I was staring at my wedding ring swaying in front of my eyes. Trembling, I reached out my hand. Tears ran down my face. Edward gently let go of the chain when I closed my hand around it. I threw myself into his arms, sobbing even harder. He stood there without reacting.

"Thank you . . . thank you, you can't imagine . . ."

All the tension that had built up in my body over the past few days was released all at once. I clung onto Edward as if he were a lifeline. My tears couldn't stop flowing. I felt Edward's hand stroking my hair. That simple touch calmed me down and made me realize whose arms I was in.

"I'm sorry," I said, moving slightly away from him.

"You should put it back on."

My hands were shaking so much that I couldn't fasten it.

"Let me help you."

He took the chain, opened it, and put his arms around my neck. My hand immediately found the ring, and I squeezed it with all my might. Edward stepped back, and for a few seconds, we stood there looking at each other.

"I'll leave you alone," he said, passing his hand over his face.

"Can I offer you something to drink?"

"No. I have work to do. Another time."

I didn't even have time to reply before he was gone.

I went to visit Abby and Jack to thank them for their help. They had been very discreet about the situation. Dealing with Judith when I spoke to her on the phone was another matter. She couldn't understand why I hadn't told her before. I got the feeling that she was more or less managing to control her curiosity. But I still hadn't found the nerve to thank my neighbor the way I should.

I was sitting on the beach in the fresh air when I saw Postman Pat trotting towards me. He came over so I could pet him, then curled up at my feet. He got there just at the right moment; I was starting to freeze and he was already warming me up.

"Tell me: do you think you could help me out? I don't really know what to say to your master. He saved my life again and I don't want to seem ungrateful. Any ideas?"

He put his head between his paws and closed his eyes.

"So you're no more talkative than he is, eh?"

"Hello," said a hoarse voice behind me.

How long had he been there?

"Hello."

"If he's annoying you, push him off."

"No, quite the opposite."

Edward smiled a little. I was sure he'd heard everything. He bent down and put a bag on the ground. He took out a camera, lit a cigarette, and handed me the pack without saying a word. I took one and got up all my courage.

"I wanted to thank you."

"That's OK."

"No, I want to do something for you. Tell me what."

"You're stubborn. But since you're insisting, you can buy me a beer at the pub tonight."

He stood up and started walking towards the sea.

"See you later," was all he said.

I'd been parked in front of the pub for fifteen minutes. Edward was already inside. I couldn't seem to get out of my car. I was preparing myself to have a drink with my sworn enemy. Sure, he had returned my wedding ring, but that alone didn't wipe the slate clean. I would have liked to be certain that we wouldn't end up in a fistfight. When I pushed open the pub door, I saw him sitting at the counter, a beer in front of him, reading the paper. I went over and stood beside him. He didn't notice I was there.

"Am I going to have to tear it out of your hands again?" I asked.

"I didn't think you'd have the nerve to show up."

"That's because you don't know me."

He gestured to the barman who came over. Edward handed him his empty pint glass and ordered two more. I didn't have time to react when he paid instead of me. Judith had warned me that her brother was macho.

This wasn't good, not good at all. I couldn't face a pint of Guinness. I'd already noticed that all the Irish women drank it, but I wasn't Irish. I was a little Parisian who had absolutely no doubt that Guinness was disgusting. But my stomach had already suffered their cheap wine, so it could cope with their draft beer. And I had no choice. Out of the question to come off as difficult with this guy.

"What are we drinking to?" I asked.

"To our truce."

I braced myself and took a sip. Then another.

"This slop is good," I said to myself. "It tastes like coffee."

"I'm sorry, I didn't understand; you were speaking French."

"Nothing, forget it."

The silence between us made me feel ill at ease.

"Are you happy with the photos you took today?"

"Not really."

"Don't you get fed up with always taking pictures of the same thing?"

"It's never the same."

He launched into a lecture on photography. He seemed in raptures over his profession. I was interested by what he was saying and was the first to be surprised by that.

"Can you make a living out of it?"

"I do a lot of bread and butter work, but I try my best to concentrate on what I like. What about you, what did you do in Paris?"

I took a deep breath and sighed before ordering another round. This time, I paid before he could. In two hours, I'd become addicted to Guinness. I took a long drink.

"I ran a literary café."

"With your husband?"

"No. Colin helped me get it started, but Felix is my business partner."

"Really? The clown I fought with?"

"The very same. But tell me, didn't that clown leave you with a little souvenir of his trip?"

I pointed at the cut that Edward still had on his

lip. To tell the truth, Felix had greatly exaggerated his exploits.

"We were both pretty ridiculous," Edward said with a smile. "So you mean that Felix is running a literary café right now?"

"Yes. He's been the only one running it for a year and a half."

"You must be close to bankruptcy, no? I'm not saying he isn't a nice guy, but I can't imagine he's a very good manager or administrator."

"You're not wrong. But it's also partly my responsibility. I haven't made an effort to take back the reins, and even before Colin and Clara died, I didn't kill myself at work."

"You'll go back there one day, of course. I imagine you have to be damned lucky to have a literary café in the center of Paris . . ."

I avoided looking at him.

We went outside the pub together with the same habit: to light a cigarette. The peace pipe. Edward walked me back to my car before getting into his.

I took an unbelievable amount of time to get the engine started; that's how surprised I was by the turn the day had taken. The sound of a car horn brought me back to reality. Edward's car was next to mine. I lowered the window.

"I'll go ahead of you," he said, with a little smile.

"Be my guest."

He sped off. When I arrived at the cottage, I told myself, for the first time, that the lights from my neighbor's house weren't annoying.

Ever since Edward and I had buried the hatchet, we continually ran into each other: on the beach, at Abby and Jack's house, where I went more and more often, and even sometimes at the pub.

I was walking along the beach. I'd lured away Postman Pat while Edward was taking pictures. As I was walking back to him, I saw him quickly put away all his equipment.

"What are you doing?"

"I don't feel like getting soaked; I'm going home."

"You're such a sissy."

He smiled at me.

"You should do the same."

"You're kidding." I looked up at the sky. "There are only three little clouds."

"You've been living here for six months and you still don't understand the weather. I promise you there's going to be a serious storm."

He gave me a wave and headed for home. Postman Pat hesitated between going with his master or staying with me. I threw a stick for him and he stayed to play.

But the game didn't last long. A downpour hit us less than fifteen minutes later. I ran back towards the cottages with the dog ahead. One day, I'll stop smoking and then I'll be able to really sprint. Edward's door was open and Postman Pat ran inside. Without thinking, I followed him, then stood dead still at the doorway when I saw Edward.

"Come in," he said. "I won't bite."

"No, I'll go home."

"Aren't you soaked enough? You want to get even wetter?"

I nodded in agreement.

"Come in and get warm.'

He went upstairs. His place still looked like a shambles. I went straight over to the fireplace to warm my hands. I was fascinated by a photo on the windowsill: a photo of a woman sitting on the beach in Mulranny. If Edward had taken that picture, he really was talented.

"Put that on," he said, coming up behind me.

I caught the sweater he threw me. It came down to my knees. Edward handed me a cup of coffee. I happily accepted and remained standing next to the fire. Then I turned back to study the photo again.

"Don't keep standing there."

"Is this one of your photos?"

"Yes. I took it just before I decided to come and live here."

"Who's the woman?"

"No one."

I turned around and leaned against the mantle. Edward sat down on one of his couches.

"How long have you been living in Mulranny?"

He bent down to pick up his cigarettes from the coffee table. After lighting one, he propped his elbows up against his knees and stroked his beard.

"Five years."

"Why did you leave Dublin?"

"Is this an interrogation?"

"No . . . no . . . I'm sorry, I'm too nosy."

I started taking off the sweater.

"What are you doing?" Edward asked.

"It's stopped raining. I won't bother you any longer."

"Don't you want to know why I became a hermit?"

I put my head back into the top of the sweater, which meant "yes".

"In truth, I left Dublin because I couldn't stand the city any more."

"But Judith said you liked it there and I thought you liked living near her."

"I needed to start a new life."

He shut up like a clam and suddenly stood up.

"Are you staying for dinner?"

Once I got over my surprise, I accepted his offer. Edward got going in the kitchen and absolutely forbade me to help him.

During the meal, he told me about Judith, his parents, and his aunt and uncle. I confided in him about my relationship with my family that was getting more and more confrontational. He had the decency not to ask me anything about Colin and Clara.

I started to look as tired as I felt.

"Now who's the sissy?" Edward asked.

"It's time for me to go home."

Edward walked me to the door. I noticed a small suitcase on the floor.

"Are you going away?"

"Tomorrow morning; I have an assignment in Belfast."

"What are you doing with your dog?"

"Do you want him?"

"If that helps you out."

"Take him; he's yours."

I opened the door and managed to whistle for Postman Pat who came trotting out. Edward petted him but it was more like thumping him. After taking a few steps away, I turned towards him.

"When will you be back?"

"In a week."

"OK. Good night."

*

The weather had been horrible all day long and we'd hardly dared venture outside. I amused myself by cooking; I'd felt like it, the urge just came over me like that. And it was also convenient having a living garbage can at my disposal.

My dinner was simmering on the stove. I was comfortably settled on the couch, the dog at my feet, a glass of wine on the side table, engrossed in *The Good Life* by Jay McInerney with piano music in the background. My peace was broken by someone knocking at the front door. Postman Pat didn't move; he was no more eager than I was to be disturbed. Still, I went and opened the door and found Edward standing there.

"Hello," he said.

"I hadn't realized you were coming back tonight."

"I can go away again, if you want."

"Idiot. Come in."

He followed me into the living room where the dog deigned to show he was glad to see him before quickly going to sprawl down in his spot. Edward started looking all around.

"Are you taking the grand tour?" I asked.

"Not at all; it's just been a long time since I was here."

"Please, make yourself at home."

"I wouldn't dare."

"Would you like a drink?"

"I'd love one."

I went into the kitchen. I used the opportunity to check the food in my pressure cooker. I'd made enough for three. I leaned against the stove to keep control. Then I went back to join Edward and handed him his glass without saying a word.

"Are you OK?" he asked.

"Do you want to stay and have dinner with me?"

"I don't know . . ."

I lit a cigarette and stood in front of the bay window. It was so dark that you couldn't see a thing outside.

"I cooked today for the first time in a year and a half and I'm still in the habit of cooking for a family. I have enough for an army. I'd like you to stay and have dinner with me."

"It would be rude to refuse."

"Thank you," I said, lowering my eyes.

Edward told me about his week over dinner. I made him laugh when I told him all the problems I'd had with his dog running away. Every now and again, I felt I was standing outside the scene, watching myself sharing a meal with the person I had called "my bastard of a neighbor" just a few weeks before. It was surreal.

After putting on the coffee, I went back into the living room and found Edward standing in the middle of the room, smoking a cigarette. I couldn't see what he was holding in his hands and staring at. He looked up and stared straight into my eyes.

"You made a beautiful family."

I walked over to him and took the picture from him. I sat down and he crouched down next to me. It was one of our last family photos, taken a few weeks before they died.

"Let me introduce Colin and Clara," I said, stroking my daughter's face.

"She looks like you."

"Do you think so?"

"I'll let you get some sleep."

He stood and put on his jacket, whistled for the dog, and headed for the front door.

"I'm leaving in three days for the Aran Islands," he said. Then he hesitated.

"Do you want me to take care of Postman Pat?"

"No. Come with me."

"What?"

"Come with me. You won't be disappointed."

And with that, he left.

7

I didn't have to think about it for long before accepting Edward's offer. We left after delivering Postman Pat to Abby and Jack, who stared at us, dumbfounded.

The car journey and ferry crossing were spent in utter silence. With him, I learned not to speak unless I really had something to say.

We had barely set foot on the island when he dragged me to one of its farthest points where he claimed the light was perfect for his photos. It was then that I began to seriously regret having come along with him. I'd always suffered from fear of heights and we were at the edge of a cliff nearly three hundred feet high.

"I wanted to show you this spot. It's restful, don't you think?" he asked.

Terrifying seemed more appropriate.

"It gives you the feeling of being alone in the world."

"That's why I like it here."

"At least you don't have any annoying neighbors."

We looked at each other then, and the expression in our eyes was full of meaning.

"I'm going to get to work," Edward said, "but you have to stay here and honor the tradition of the island."

"What are you talking about?"

"Everyone who comes here has to lie flat on his stomach and lean his head down over the edge. Your turn to play!"

He started to walk away but I grabbed his arm to hold him back.

"Are you kidding?"

"Are you afraid?"

"Oh, no, not at all, quite the opposite," I replied stiffly. "I love getting a thrill."

"Well, have fun then."

This time, he really did leave. He was daring me. I smoked a cigarette. Then I got down on my knees. The only way I could get near the edge was to crawl. Like on a commando training course. I started shaking about three feet from my goal. My muscles seized up; I was paralyzed, and I was close to screaming in terror. Time passed and I was incapable of standing up to back away from the precipice. Moving my head to see where Edward was taking pictures seemed impossible; I would surely fall. I whispered his name so he would come and rescue me. To no avail.

"Edward," I called loudly. "Come here, please."

The minutes seemed like hours. Finally, Edward came over to me.

"What are you still doing here?"

"Having tea, what does it look like?"

"Don't tell me you're afraid of heights?"

"Well, I am."

"Then why did you want to do this?"

"It doesn't matter. Do something, anything, pull me back by my feet, but don't leave me here."

"I don't think so."

The bastard. I felt him stretching out beside me.

"What are you doing?"

Without saying a word, he moved closer to me, put an arm around my back, and held me close. I still didn't move.

"Move forward with me," he said quietly.

"No," I whispered.

When I felt Edward starting to move towards the edge, I hid my head against his neck.

"I'll fall."

"I won't let go of you."

I slowly looked up at him. The wind whipped my face and my hair was flying in all directions. I gradually opened my eyes and felt like I was being sucked into a void when I saw the waves beating against the rock face. Edward tightened his grip. I half closed my eyes, giving in; I couldn't control anything, my whole body went limp. I turned towards Edward. He was watching me.

"What?" I asked.

"Enjoy the view."

I glanced at him once more before leaning out again. Edward stood up, grabbed me by the waist, and pulled me up. I gave him a little smile.

"Let's go," he said, putting one arm around my back.

We spent the evening at the pub in the port. On the way to the bed and breakfast where we were staying, I found out he'd be leaving early the next morning; he wanted to take some pictures at sunrise.

I stretched out in my bed; I'd slept like a baby. It was already quite late in the day. When I got up, I noticed a piece of paper had been slipped under my door. There was a map of the island and a note for me. Edward told me where he'd be spending the day.

The owner served me a gigantic breakfast. While wolfing it down, I listened to him tell me about Edward and the times he'd been there by himself.

A little later, I'd nearly reached my goal: I'd been walking for more than an hour across the heath. The beach was right ahead of me; I could see Edward in the distance, holding his camera. If

I hadn't been afraid of breaking his concentration, I think I would have run over to him, without quite knowing why. I sat down and watched him. I took a handful of sand and played with it. I felt good; I could breathe again. Life was reasserting itself and I didn't want to fight it any more.

Edward walked back from the beach, his bag over his shoulder, smoking a cigarette. When he got to me, he sat down beside me.

"So the sleepyhead finally woke up?"

I lowered my eyes and smiled. I felt him move closer. He kissed me on the forehead.

"Hello," was all he said.

I was flustered.

"So, how are the pictures?" I asked to change the subject.

"I won't know until I see the proofs. I'm done for today. Do you want to go for a little walk?" he suggested, standing up.

I looked up at him. I stared at him and wanted to hold his hand; nothing was stopping me. He held me close. I stood there for a few moments, over-whelmed by the sense of security that washed over me. Finally, I gently pulled away. I walked towards the sea and when I looked back, Edward was behind me. I smiled at him, and he smiled back.

I'd slept for half the day, and I was still exhausted. I was going to collapse into a heap again.

"What do you have planned for tomorrow?" I asked Edward as we stood in front of the door to my room.

"I found a boat so I could spend the day on another island in the open seas."

"Can I go with you?"

He smiled, then wiped his face with his hand.

"Never mind. I'll just get in your way," I said, opening the door to my room.

"I didn't say no."

I turned around and looked at him.

"Come with me, but you'll have to get up at dawn."

He gave me a wry smile.

"Hey! I'm capable of getting up early!"

"In that case, I'll come and get you at six o'clock."

He came closer and just as he had that afternoon, he kissed me on the forehead.

I'd set the alarm clock in the room and the one on my phone. When they both went off at once, I leaped out of bed. I felt like I'd hardly had any sleep. I thought I would collapse with exhaustion in the shower. I was running on automatic when I opened my door at exactly six o'clock. Through half-opened eyes, I saw Edward, bright as a button.

"What planet are you from?" I asked him, sounding groggy.

"I don't sleep very much."

"Are there bunks on the boat?"

He gestured me to follow him. He made a detour to the kitchen while I leaned against the wall at the entrance wondering how I was going to make it through the day.

"Here," he said.

I opened my eyes. He handed me a thermos.

"Is this really what I think it is?"

"I'm getting to know you."

"Thank you! Thank God!" I followed him out to the car.

My dose of caffeine and what I saw when we got to the port finally woke me up. You could hear the sound of the trawlers and see the night mist thanks to the lights on the fishing boats. I quickly realized we were about to get into one of those old tubs. All I needed was a yellow wax jacket and navy blue boots to be the very picture of a Parisian at sea. I stayed back while Edward said hello to the sailors. They all had a cigarette hanging from their lips and faces deeply lined by the elements. Forces of nature. I felt particularly uncomfortable when they all turned to look at me. Edward waved at me to come over and get on the boat.

"You're going to stay on the bridge," he said.

"And what about you?"

"I'm going with them."

"All right."

"Don't move from there; I'll come and get you. And umm . . . don't touch anything and don't say anything."

"I can hold my own."

"Don't you know the old saying? A woman on a boat is bad luck. And since they didn't know you were coming, I had a battle to keep you with me."

"What did you say to convince them?"

He looked at me, suddenly very serious, and wiped his face with his hand.

"Nothing special."

He walked away.

Since I hadn't caused any problems on the crossing, I was treated to a few smiles when I got off the boat.

After spending the morning at the port with the trawler men, we headed towards the beach. It was actually an inlet surrounded by high cliffs. Edward got to work, and I took the opportunity to go and explore what was hidden behind the rocks. I climbed up. Nothing but the sea on the horizon. I leaned against the rocks and closed my eyes. A ray of sunlight warmed me up, and I enjoyed the moment.

"Diane!" Edward called, from behind me.

"Yes?"

I glanced at him and my smile faded when I realized he'd just taken my picture. He looked very satisfied with himself and walked away. I hurried down from my rock to run after him.

"Show me those pictures right now!"

"Artistic property," he replied, lifting his camera out of reach.

I ran all around him, trying to jump high enough to grab it, but in vain. I finally collapsed down on the sand and Edward did the same.

"Will I see them one day?"

"If you're a good girl."

He'd left the camera on the ground. In a flash, I jumped over him, stole the object of my desire, and took off as fast as a rabbit. Thinking I had a few fractions of a second to spare, I turned it around to see it from all sides.

"How do you turn this thing on?"

"Like this."

Edward was right behind me. He put his arms around me, took my hands and guided me. The screen lit up.

"Do you really want to see them now?" he whispered in my ear.

"On one condition."

"I'm listening."

"I want some pictures with you in them."

"I hate that."

"Is the gentleman photographer afraid to have his picture taken?"

He didn't reply, just started fiddling with the settings on the camera. His face was leaning over my shoulder and he looked deep in thought. He finally raised his arm and took the picture without warning me.

"Smile, Edward. Wait, I'll help you."

I turned around to face him, still in his arms. He frowned. I held his face and pulled his mouth into a smile.

"You see, you can when you want to! Go on then, get to work!"

It was the first time I saw Edward so joyful, almost carefree. He had me climb onto his back for a series of pictures. I was thrashing about so much that we ended up falling. I managed to snatch the camera from him and run away. When I turned around, I saw that Edward hadn't moved. He was watching me. He sat down, lit a cigarette, looked away, and stared out into the distance. By some miracle, I brought the camera up quickly and managed to immortalize the scene. I went back and stood in front of him.

"Well, what's your professional opinion?"

He stuck his cigarette in the corner of his mouth, took the camera from my hand, and leaned over it. He looked up at me when he realized he was the subject of the photo.

"Come here," he said, pointing to the space between his knees.

I slid down in front of him; he put his arms around me and showed me the screen.

"It's not bad at all for a first try," he said. "But you see, there, it needs . . ."

I couldn't hear what he was saying any more. I turned to stare up at him and it was as if I were seeing him for the first time: his messy hair, his beard, the color of his eyes. I breathed in his scent for the first time, too, a mixture of soap and stale tobacco. I was so overcome with emotion that I had to close my eyes.

"Let's take one more little picture."

I saw he was looking at me. He put the camera down without taking his eyes off me. He put one hand against my cheek. I leaned my face against his palm.

"We should get back to the port; the boat won't wait for us," he said, his voice more husky than usual.

He stood up, gathered together his equipment, and helped me up. We walked hand in hand for a long time on the way back.

"Wake up, we're here."

It was Edward's voice. He had stayed with me below deck and I'd fallen asleep in his arms during the crossing. He stroked my cheek to help me come around. I rubbed my face against his. I felt good.

The owner of the bed and breakfast was there to greet us, despite the late hour. He'd saved us some leftovers for dinner. Edward was right at home here. He heated up the food and poured us a drink while I sat on a high bar stool and watched him, without doing anything. Once we sat down, all we did was look at each other; we didn't say a word.

"You haven't forgotten that we're going back to Mulranny tomorrow, have you?" Edward asked me after dinner, while we were smoking a cigarette outside.

"I'd stopped thinking about it," I replied, suddenly feeling a heaviness in my stomach.

"Are you all right?"

"I feel free here. I don't want to go back."

"Let's go to bed."

He held the door open for me and I walked ahead, brushing against him; he followed me up to my room. I paused in the hallway. When I turned around, I was surprised at how close he was to me. His head was down and he had one hand pressed high against the wall.

"Thank you for these three days."

"I was happy to have you with me."

He looked deep into my eyes. My heart was racing. He moved closer to me, put his lips against my forehead, and lingered there. I couldn't fight it any longer. I clutched his shirt. He stepped back a little and leaned down towards me. Our foreheads brushed against each other. I couldn't control my breathing any more; my stomach was in knots. His lips brushed against mine once, then again. He put his arms around me and kissed me passionately; I returned his kiss. When we finally stopped kissing, he leaned his forehead against mine and stroked my cheek.

"Stop me," he whispered. "Please."

I lowered my eyes and saw I was still gripping his shirt. All my senses were aroused, but I had to work out how I felt. Reluctantly, I let go of his shirt and, as gently as possible, pushed him away. He let me, a little too easily.

"I'm sorry," he said. "I . . ."

I put my finger against his lips to silence him.

"I think it's better if we leave it here, for tonight."

I kissed the corner of his mouth. I opened the door and went into my room. I turned towards him; he was watching my every move.

"Sleep well," I whispered.

He wiped his face with one hand, smiled at me, and took two steps back. I silently closed the door and leaned against it. It was only at that very moment that I realized my legs were shaking. I listened for noises in the house; I heard Edward go back downstairs. I smiled; he'd gone for a cigarette, I was sure of it.

Still shaken, I slipped under my duvet. In the half-light, I ran my fingers across my lips. I'd liked feeling his lips on mine. I could have gone further but hadn't. Moving too fast, perhaps. I settled down in the middle of the bed. In spite of my heavy eyes, I stared at the ray of light under the door. Then I heard footsteps on the staircase; they stopped in front of my door.

I sat up. Edward was there, very close. I got out of bed, trying to think fast about what I should do. I'd decided to open the door for him when I heard him go into his room. Total darkness now; I stretched out in bed again. As sleep overtook me, I told myself that I would see Edward the next day. I couldn't wait.

I opened my eyes and my first thoughts were of him. I looked at my watch; our boat was leaving in an hour. I got showered and dressed, packed my things, and closed my bag. In the hallway, I glanced over at his room; the door was open. I went to see if he was still inside. No one. The room had already been cleaned. I went into the kitchen. Only the owner was there. He smiled at me and gave me a cup of coffee. He was about to give me one of his breakfasts, which seemed to be his specialty.

"No, thank you. I'm not very hungry this morning."

"As you like, but it's better to have something in your stomach for the crossing."

"I'll be fine with the coffee."

I took a few sips, still standing.

"Have you seen Edward?" I asked.

"He rushed out early. Even less talkative than usual, can you imagine that?"

"Hard to believe."

"He went down to the port, then came back to pay your bills."

"And where is he now?"

"Pacing like a lion trapped in a cage; he's waiting for you outside."

"Oh . . ."

I gulped down the rest of my coffee under the mocking eye of my host.

"You're all white. Is it because of the crossing or Edward?"

"Which is worse?"

He burst out laughing.

I gave him a little wave to say goodbye and

walked towards the front door.

Edward didn't notice me. His face a blank, he was smoking a cigarette like a maniac. I softly called his name. He turned around, stared at me with a vacant expression, and walked over to me. Without a word, he picked up my bag. I took his arm to hold him back.

"How are you?"

"And you?" he asked dryly.

"Fine, at least I think so."

"Let's go."

He smiled slightly, took my hand, and led me to the port. The longer we walked, the closer I stood to him. In the end, our fingers were interlocked.

We had to let go of each other when we got to the boat, so he could load the bags. I followed him onto the deck. There was a fierce, howling wind. He lit a cigarette, handed it to me, then I watched him light one for himself. He was leaning against the rails. We smoked in silence.

The boat left the island. We hadn't moved.

"It's going to start rocking," Edward told me, standing up.

"Are you staying here?"

"For now. Go inside if you like."

I got my footing and grabbed onto the railing like him. The boat was already pitching, and the wind was hurting my ears, but nothing in the world would have made me want to be anywhere else. Suddenly, I was being sheltered. Edward had gone to stand behind me; he put his arms around me and his hands over mine.

"Tell me if you feel sick," he whispered in my ear.

There was laughter in his voice; I elbowed him gently in the ribs.

We spent the whole crossing holding each other tight and not saying a word. It felt so good to make the most of it, just the two of us. When the boat reached the quayside, Edward went to get our bags. He held my hand again as we walked towards the parking lot. He loaded the trunk while I got in the car. When he climbed in, he sighed deeply. He must have felt me watching him; he turned towards me and looked straight into my eyes.

"Are we going home?"

"You're the driver."

Throughout the whole journey, we each sat engrossed in our own thoughts, lulled by music by the Red Hot Chili Peppers, a mixture of sweetness and brutality, just like Edward. The only sound was the cigarette lighter. We took turns lighting cigarettes. The countryside sped past my eyes; I fiddled with my necklace and wedding ring. I didn't dare look at Edward now. When I saw the sign for Mulranny, my whole body tensed. He parked the car in front of my cottage but left the motor running.

"Well, I've got work to do."

"No problem," I replied quickly as I got out of the car.

I slammed the door harder than I'd intended. I got my bags out of the trunk. Edward didn't move and still hadn't driven away. When I got to the door of my cottage, I started fishing around for my key. By the time I finally found it, I was so furious that I couldn't get it into the lock. If he had nothing to say to me, all he had to do was leave.

I dropped everything and suddenly turned around. I bumped straight into Edward. He caught me and put an arm around my waist so I didn't fall backwards. Several seconds passed. Then he let go of me. I ran my hand through my hair; he lit a cigarette.

"Would you come to my place tonight?" he asked.

"I . . . yes . . . I'd like that."

We looked at each other for a long time. The tension was mounting. Edward slowly nodded.

"See you later."

I frowned when I saw him lean over. He picked up my key and opened the door.

"It's better that way, don't you think?"

He kissed my forehead and walked back to his car before I had a chance to say a word. I watched his Land Rover take off in a cloud of dust.

8

I'd just gotten out of a long, steamy, relaxing shower. I stood naked in front of the mirror and looked at my body. It had been a very long time since I'd cared about it. My body had died along with Colin. Edward had gently awakened it last night. I knew what would happen between us tonight. Up until now, I'd thought that no man would ever touch me again. Would I let Edward's hands and body replace Colin's? I mustn't think about that. All my past feminine habits came back to me: applying moisturizer, putting a drop of perfume between my breasts, combing my hair, choosing my underwear, dressing with a desire to be seductive.

Night had fallen. I was in a real state, self-conscious, like some teenager in love, but over a man I'd only recently hated. And now, a few hours without him and I missed him. I glanced out the window; the lights were on in his house. Instead of biting my nails, I smoked a cigarette. I wandered around the room, feeling suddenly very hot, then shivering with cold. Why wait any longer? I put on my leather jacket, grabbed my bag and left. Even though our cottages were only a few yards apart, I still found a way to light another cigarette. I stopped halfway there, told myself I could just turn around and he wouldn't know; I'd call him and tell him I wasn't feeling well. I was terrified; I was bound to disappoint him, I didn't know how to make love any more. I laughed at myself. Ridiculous, that's what I was. It was like riding a bike, you don't forget how. I stubbed out my cigarette and knocked on his door. Edward took a few seconds to answer it. He looked me up and down, then stared deep into my eyes.

I started breathing quickly, and the appearance of calm I'd hoped to give him went up in smoke.

"Come in."

"Thanks," I replied, very softly.

He stepped back to let me pass. Postman Pat greeted me enthusiastically but that didn't relax me in the least. I jumped when I felt Edward's hand on my back. He led me into the living room.

"Would you like a drink?"

"Yes, please."

He kissed my forehead and went behind the bar. Rather than watch his every move, I looked around to convince myself that this was the same Edward from before our trip to the Aran Islands, that we were going to spend a completely normal, friendly evening together, that I'd been inventing what had happened between us. His notoriously messy place and overflowing ashtrays would reassure me. I looked around several times, feeling even more panicky as I realized something was different.

"You cleaned up?"

"Are you surprised?"

"Maybe. I'm not sure."

"Come and sit down."

I glanced over in his direction. He gestured for me to sit down on the couch. I perched on the edge. I took the glass of wine he handed me without looking at him. I had to find some way—any way—to overcome my nerves. I took out a cigarette and didn't have time to get out my lighter before a flame appeared in front of me. I thanked Edward.

He sat on the coffee table facing me, drank some Guinness, and looked at me. I dropped my head. He lifted my chin up.

"Is everything all right?"

"Of course. What did you do today? Did you work? What were the pictures like? You know, the ones we took together."

My monologue had left me breathless. Edward stroked my cheek.

"Relax."

I gave a great sigh.

"I'm sorry."

I jumped up and walked around the room before stopping next to the fireplace. I finished my cigarette and threw the butt into the fire. I could feel

Edward standing behind me. He took my glass, set it down on the mantle and put his arms around me. I stiffened.

"What are you afraid of?"

"Everything . . ."

"You have nothing to fear with me."

I turned around to look at him. He smiled at me, pushing my hair off my face. I fell into his arms. I breathed in his scent. He stroked my back. We stayed like that for a long time. I felt good. All my doubts disappeared. I gently kissed him. He took my face in his hands and leaned his forehead against mine.

"You know that I nearly turned back when I was coming over here?"

"Then you nearly got yourself torn to pieces."

"You mean you would have come over and demanded an explanation?"

"You'd better believe it."

I was fiddling with a button on his shirt.

"I thought about you all day long."

I looked up at him and he held my gaze. It was up to me to decide how far we would go. That was the moment I asked my brain to switch off; my body was taking the lead. I stood on tiptoe.

"I trust you," I said, pressing my lips to his.

I kissed him the way I thought I would never kiss anyone again. He grabbed my hips and crushed me against him. I clung onto his shoulders. I felt his hands reaching under my clothes, touching my back, my stomach, my breasts. His caresses made me feel more confident; I pulled his shirt out of his jeans and unbuttoned it. I wanted to feel his skin, feel his warm, living flesh. We only stopped kissing long enough for Edward to take off my T-shirt. We looked at each other. He lifted me up and I wrapped my legs around his waist. Then he lay us down on the couch. I gave a sigh of pleasure at the feel of our naked flesh touching, pressing against each other. I felt his beard tickling my neck; he kissed my ear.

"Are you sure?" he whispered.

I looked at him, stroked his hair, smiled, and kissed him. At that very moment, the dog started growling, which was a little unsettling.

"Bed," Edward ordered.

We both looked in his direction. He was snarling,

still growling and staring at the front door. Edward put his fingers against my lips so I wouldn't say anything. Someone was knocking at the door.

"You should go and see," I whispered. "It might be important."

"We've got better things to do."

He pressed his lips to mine while unbuttoning my jeans. I had no desire to stop him.

"Edward, I know you're in there!" a woman's voice shouted through the door.

It was an order. Edward closed his eyes and his face hardened. He started to get up but I held him back.

"Who is it?"

"Open the door," the woman cried impatiently. "I need to speak to you."

He pulled away and got up. I sat on the couch, covered my breasts with my arms and watched him. He rubbed his face and ruffled his hair, as if he were trying to wake himself up. Then he lit a cigarette and picked his shirt up from the floor.

"What's going on?" I asked, quietly.

"Get dressed."

His voice was harsh. Tears in my eyes, I went to find my T-shirt and bra. As soon as I was dressed, he went to the front door without even looking at me. He shoved Postman Pat out of the way so he could get by. The dog came and hid against my legs. Edward grabbed the doorknob so hard that his veins stood out. Then he opened it. The entrance was hidden by his body, but I could hear everything.

"Megan," he said.

"My God, I'm so happy to see you. I've missed you so much."

She threw her arms around his neck. This was some kind of bad joke. I coughed; I couldn't help myself. Edward's body tensed. The woman raised her eyes, saw me, pulled away from him, and moved back.

She was gorgeous, slender, with a good figure, and looking wide-eyed at him. Long black hair flowed down her back. Her demeanor and bearing were very feminine, and very studied. Her features were arrogant, and she reeked of self-confidence. She looked back and forth at us. Edward had turned towards me, his eyes blank. He seemed to be somewhere else, somewhere hellish. She ran her fingers through his hair. He didn't react.

"I see I got here just in time," she said.

Then she walked over to me.

"Whoever you are, it's time to leave us alone."

I paid no attention to her; I walked over to Edward. I tried to take his hand but he pulled away.

"Say something. Who is this?"

He stared into space and sighed.

"I'm his wife," she said, putting her arm through his.

"Megan," Edward cut in sharply.

"I'm sorry, my love, I know."

"What the hell is going on?" I said angrily.

For the first time since the woman had arrived, Edward looked into my eyes. He was cold and distant; he wasn't the same man any more. He was even more frightening than when I first got to Mulranny. I recoiled in pain. At that moment, I glanced over at the mantle and saw the photo. I understood. The woman on the beach was not no one. What a fool I'd been. He'd really taken me for a ride. I picked up my bag and jacket and walked out of the cottage without bothering to close the door or look back.

I had to stop on the way home to throw up. Once inside, I took a long shower to scrub myself clean of any trace of that bastard from my body. I'd been that close to sleeping with a married man. It hadn't even occurred to me to ask him if there was anyone else. I'd simply assumed that if he wanted to be with me, it meant he was free. In fact, I was just a stand-in. What would Colin think from where he was? All it had taken was two or three smiles and a romantic weekend for me to be willing to spread my legs. I was disgusted with myself.

Impossible to fall asleep, so I sat down in front of my bedroom window, in the dark, folded my legs under me, and rocked backed and forth. I finally fell asleep and had terrible dreams all night long. Edward's and Colin's faces merged in my dreams, conspiring against me.

I hadn't left the house in three days. I couldn't sleep at all any more and kept going over and over the past few weeks I'd spent with Edward. I wanted to figure out exactly what had gone wrong, exactly when I'd decided to close my eyes and ears about the main topic: Mrs. Edward.

I'd forced myself to go and do the shopping and had managed to go unrecognized at the grocery store. I was closing the trunk of my car.

"Diane?"

I recognized Jack's voice. My body drooped; I put on a false smile and turned around.

"So how's our little Frenchwoman? It's been a long time since we've seen you."

"Hello, Jack. I'm fine, thanks."

"Follow me back home, Abby would love to see you."

And she was. As soon as I went inside, she threw her arms around my neck. The warmth they showed me cooled my anger. I felt comfortable with them, so I answered their gentle questions and soon found myself talking about Clara.

"Do you think you'll go back to France one day?" Abby cut in.

"I haven't thought about that yet."

"Don't you want to pick up the life you had back there?"

"Do you need the cottage?"

"No."

They couldn't fool me. They were lying. There it was: the Frenchwoman was getting in the way and should make way for Edward's wife. The front door opened and closed. I froze.

"You've turned completely white all of a sudden. Aren't you feeling well?"

"I'm just suddenly feeling tired, nothing serious; I'll go home now."

"Ask Edward to take you back."

"Definitely not," I said, my voice rising. "I'll be fine."

I hurriedly stood up and picked up my things.

"See you soon," I called before running towards the door.

I passed Edward in the hallway. I couldn't look at him. He didn't try to speak to me. I locked myself in my car and collapsed over the steering wheel. I was afraid, afraid of him and afraid of my reaction.

*

I was sitting in front of my bay window and saw Edward walking along the beach with his dog. I knew I'd have to confront him at some point; I needed an explanation. I wanted proof that I hadn't imagined it all.

A trip to the bathroom was required. Out of the question to give him the satisfaction of seeing me look a wreck. I took particular care in choosing my clothes and putting on makeup to hide my nights of insomnia.

Impossible to back out now; I'd just knocked on his door and I could hear Postman Pat barking. It seemed an eternity until he answered: my hands were cold, I was shivering, and there was a knot in my stomach. All these symptoms disappeared when Edward opened the door. A feeling of anger rushed through me. I wanted to hit him with all my might, but what really made me furious was my desire to kiss him and fall into his arms. I hadn't expected to feel those emotions, and the beautiful speech I'd practiced in front of my mirror vanished into thin air.

"What do you want?"

"Hello," I stammered.

He sighed and ran one hand across his face.

"Hurry up, I have things to do." I stood up tall, shoulders back, and looked straight at him.

"You owe me an explanation."

His face was full of surprise, then anger.

"I owe you nothing at all."

"How can you look at yourself in the mirror?"

He looked at me darkly and slammed the door in my face. One of his old habits.

In spite of the low sky and threatening clouds, I decided to get some fresh air. I walked back and forth along the beach for more than an hour. When I was heading back to my cottage, I saw Postman Pat running towards me. I petted him before continuing on my way. I didn't want to stay there. A car pulled up in front of Edward's house. His wife got out just as I was passing. I could feel her watching me.

"So you're still here, are you?"

I lowered my head and stopped myself from answering her.

"I'm going to see Abby and Jack and make sure that you won't be bothering us any more."

While feeling around in my pockets for my cigarettes, I found my car keys. That was what I needed. I wasn't fast enough.

"Edward," she called.

"Coming," I heard him reply.

I slammed the car door and sped away.

For more than two hours, I drove as fast as I could, without a destination or direction. I only slowed down when I got back to the village, but not slow enough to avoid seeing Megan coming out of Jack and Abby's. She was at home everywhere. I'd thought that Mulranny would finally heal me, but instead this place was going to put me in my grave.

Judith had forgotten about me, too. She hadn't told me she was coming. And she'd been talking to Megan on the beach for an hour. When I saw her heading to my place, I quickly grabbed my bag and keys and went out.

"Diane," she called.

"I don't have time."

"What's going on with you?"

"None of your business."

"Wait," she said, grabbing hold of my arm.

"Let go of me."

I pulled free, got into my car and drove off.

I got to Mulranny after wandering along the roads for quite a long time. Since they were all at Abby and Jack's, I'd have the pub to myself. I pushed open the door, intending to get really drunk. I climbed onto a bar stool and ordered the first of many drinks to come. Ireland was going to turn me into an alcoholic.

Over the next few hours, ordering drink after drink, I went from laughing to crying. My head on the bar, I stared at the row of empty glasses. I wanted to go outside for a smoke, but fell.

Instead of crashing down onto the floor, I collapsed against someone.

"Thanks," I said to the guy who'd caught me. I'd never seen him around before.

"You're welcome. Can I offer you a cigarette?"

"You're a sly one!"

I walked towards the terrace, gesturing him to follow me. In spite of the fog in my head, I knew he was looking me up and down. Let him enjoy himself, I couldn't care less; after everything I'd gone through, it didn't matter. I went into "dumb blond" mode. I laughed like a silly fool at the jokes he told me, even though I didn't understand a word. He didn't waste any time. He put his arm around my waist to walk me back to the bar. He was staring at my cleavage. I glanced up at him; not bad. After all, one Irishman was as good as another. He might be just what I needed to exorcise Edward. I gave him an inviting look and suggested he have a drink with me. He didn't hesitate to accept.

"Can you bring us another round?" I mumbled to the barman.

"Diane, you have to stop now."

"No, bring us some drinks, I'm paying. And I have a right to have a good time!"

I threw some coins on the counter. Another drink appeared. I gulped it down and everything went blank.

I was completely out of it but I could hear voices shouting around me.

"Get away from her!"

That voice . . . I would have recognized it anywhere. Edward. Who was he shouting about like that? I opened my eyes and saw him grab the guy by his shirt collar. He said something I could barely make out.

"Wait a minute. She's the one who's been coming on to me," he said, pointing at me.

Edward's fist flew; the guy ended up on the ground. Getting shakily to his feet, he didn't hang around for more; he made a beeline for the exit.

"Oh . . . what have I done?" I said.

"It's what you nearly did that's interesting," Judith replied. I hadn't noticed her before.

"Screw you."

With those fine words, I tried to turn on my heels but it was my head that was turning, and the room was spinning dangerously.

"Hey big brother, she's trying to take off," Judith called to Edward. "Wait, Diane, we'll take you home."

"Leave me the hell alone; I can go home by myself. And keep your nose out of my business!"

I stopped. It was now or never if I wanted to make him understand what I was thinking. I tried to focus because I had not one, but two Edwards standing in front of me.

"Listen to me and listen good," I shouted. "You have no right interfering in my life. You lost that right the other night. I can sleep with whoever I . . ."

"Be quiet," he ordered. "You've already made enough of a fool of yourself."

Before I had time to reply, he picked me up and threw me over his shoulder like a sack. I beat his back with my fists and struggled.

"Put me down, you shithead."

He tightened his grip and went out to the parking lot. Without a single word, he put me in his car. I blacked out.

I woke up in my own bed. Someone had undressed me.

"You're going to have some hangover," Judith said.

"Leave me the hell alone."

"Not a chance."

She pulled the covers over me before leaving.

A few minutes later, I could hear more footsteps. I opened my eyes. Edward put a glass of water on my night table and stroked my forehead.

"Don't touch me."

I tried to sit up.

"Lie down."

Edward gently pushed me down. I was incapable of fighting him.

"This is all your fault," I said, tears rising. "You're nothing but a dirty bastard."

"I know."

I hid under the covers. I heard him rush down the stairs. Then the front door slammed.

My whole body ached. Every step I took reverberated in my head. When I got to the bathroom, I had to hold onto the sink. I was horrified by how I looked in the mirror. My face was swollen, my mascara had run under my eyes, and my hair looked like a crow's nest. I was so ashamed of myself that I didn't dare look at my wedding ring, let alone touch it. I brushed my teeth several times to try to get rid of the taste of alcohol encrusted in my mouth. One thing was sure: I was going to stop drinking.

Judith was sitting on my couch, leafing through a magazine.

"What are you still doing here?"

"Why are you so angry?"

"You win! I'm going to clear off from your shitty hellhole. You're all crazy."

"What are you talking about?"

"All of you have been laughing at me ever since I got here."

"What? We were all worried about you last night."

"You don't say."

I raised my eyes to heaven. Judith went into the kitchen while I flopped down into an armchair.

She came back five minutes later holding a tray.

"You eat and then we'll talk."

I ate my breakfast while crying. I drank my coffee and Judith refilled my cup. Then she lit a cigarette and handed it to me.

"Why didn't you tell me you were coming?" I asked.

"That's not the reason you were so pathetic last night though, was it?"

"You were the last straw. I mean, in a manner of speaking. It seems I didn't need a straw, did I? Was I really that pathetic?"

"Trust me, you don't want to know."

She raised an eyebrow; I held my head in my hands.

"Tell me what's going on. Every since I got here, I feel like I'm in a living nightmare. The slut is back, Edward is beating up any guy who goes near you, and you're acting like a bitch in heat at the pub."

I was still holding my head in my hands; I peeked through my fingers to look at her.

"What slut?"

"Megan. Who else?"

"You call your brother's wife a slut?"

"Where on earth did you get the idea she's his wife? I think I'd know if my brother was married!"

"Well, that's how she introduced herself, and he didn't deny it."

"What a jerk." She raised an eyebrow. "Wait a minute . . . there's something I don't get. You were there when she showed up at his place late that night?"

"Yes," I replied, lowering my eyes.

"Did you sleep with him?"

"We didn't get a chance."

"Shit! That bitch has some kind of radar. And Edward has no balls."

She stood up and started pacing back and forth. She was making me dizzy. I lit another cigarette and went to look out the window. I saw Edward on the beach, in the distance. I leaned my forehead against the cold glass.

"Diane."

"What?"

"Do you love him?"

I paused, my heart racing. "I think so . . . something is pushing me towards him. When we were alone together, I felt good . . . but that doesn't change anything; even if they're not married, they're together."

"No, you're wrong."

Judith crashed down on the couch, lit a cigarette, screwed up her eyes, and looked at me.

"If he finds out that I told you about it, he'll kill me. But I don't give a damn. Sit down."

I sat down.

"You know that his lousy character isn't just because our parents died. His relationship with Megan screwed up his life. That's why I came rushing over as fast as I could after Abby's panicky phone call."

"So who the hell is this woman?"

"A social climber. A shark. A bitch. She's always wanted to be successful and have some status in society, any way she could and using anyone she could. She started with nothing, made herself who she is today, worked like a dog to get where she is. She's a headhunter for the biggest recruitment agency in Dublin. She'd disown her mother and father with no problem at all to get what she wants. She's merciless, cunning, vicious, and more importantly, manipulative."

"And that's the kind of woman he likes?" I scoffed.

"I have no idea, but she's the only woman he's ever lived with."

"That woman is the love of his life?"

"In a way."

I opened my eyes wide and tried not to throw up.

"What you need to know is that before he met her, Edward didn't want to commit to anyone. He always thought that love relationships were destined to fail. To him, if you fall in love, you suffer in the end because you'll be betrayed and abandoned. So he always had relationships that were going nowhere, until the day he met her. In the beginning, he wanted her as a trophy. She let him stew. She's a real man-eater. She'd spun her web before giving in to him.

"Edward was seduced by her willpower, self-confidence, and determination. And afterwards, she stuck the knife in while pretending to be the virtuous woman who believes in love and wants to have a family . . ."

I was seething with anger; I wanted to kill someone. How could he have been taken in by such a bitch?

"But what about you? You didn't believe her?"

"I started my own little investigation about her. I didn't like the look of her. She was too worldly, too sickly sweet to be true. I found out that she'd spotted Edward and wanted him as a plaything. She told friends that his air of the dark, tortured artist would be good for her. To her, it was a way to soften her reputation as a shark. I told Edward everything and nearly lost him. We didn't speak to each other for months."

"How did it end between them?" I practically shouted.

"Calm down, Diane . . . It's a hell of a story . . . At the time, Edward was going through a period when he wasn't happy at work. He was working for a magazine but wanted to go freelance. Megan was dead against the plan. I always thought she was afraid her standard of living would drop. So, to make a long story short, my brother has always been the same, but in that situation, of course, he went to extremes. He was frustrated and terrifyingly angry. It wasn't a good idea to be in the same room with them when they were shouting and cursing each other. Though he still needed her and her support. But he behaved like an asshole and pushed her too far. You know it wouldn't take much."

I tightened my fists to contain my mounting anger and rage. I was about to erupt.

"Go on . . . " I muttered between clenched teeth.

"Edward left on an assignment. When he got back, he found her in the sack with someone she worked with."

"That's horrible!" I shouted, leaping to my feet.

"He smashed the guy's face in. He'd be dead now if it weren't for Megan pleading with Edward. Afterwards, Edward loaded all his things into his car. She begged him to stay, promised it would never happen again, that they could get through it together and that she loved him more than anything. You can imagine he wouldn't listen to a word."

I was like a caged lion, turning in circles while staring at Judith.

"Just like him, don't you think?"

"He was going to ask her to marry him as soon as his problems at work got straightened out. You can imagine the hell he went through."

"How did he pull himself together?"

"Well, you've seen how. He went to an animal shelter to get his mutt, then made his way to the

Aran Islands. He disappeared off the face of the earth for two months. No one knew where he was. I'd even started thinking about putting up a missing persons poster. Then, one day, he turned up here and asked Abby and Jack for the keys to our parents' house. And he moved in. From that moment on, he decided that no woman would ever make him suffer like that again and that he'd stay single."

"So why is Megan here? What does she want?"

"She wants him. She loves him, in her own way."

I couldn't believe it.

"She never got over him," Judith continued when she saw my astonished expression. "For five years she's done everything she can to get him back. She even came to whine at my feet. Megan's the only woman he's ever loved. In spite of everything she's done to him, I know they see each other from time to time when he goes to Dublin for work. You'd think she was having him followed! She always knows where he is. And, coincidentally, whenever they run into each other, Edward never spends the night at my place. He's like a drug addict who relapses after rehab."

"She's got him, no matter what she does," I cried bitterly.

"I'd say she used to have him. Because you arrived and you changed him. I don't know how you did it. You must have some sort of secret. He couldn't stand you at Christmas time but he took you to his refuge. The Aran Islands are like the Holy Land to him."

"A fat lot of good that does me!"

I couldn't stand still. I picked up my pack of cigarettes and lit one. I took a long drag to try to calm down.

"I'm worried about him," Judith said. "Just at the very moment when he was about to trust you, to try, Megan shows up, swearing to him by all that's holy that he's the only man she'll ever love and that she'll even come and live with him here. He's going to go crazy."

"He didn't try to stop me from going when she arrived, and he told me to get lost when I went to ask him for an explanation. To me, it's very simple: he's made his choice. She's living with him, isn't she?"

"No. He sent her to the hotel. I saw his reaction that night; he was insanely worried when the pub owner called him. And afterwards, when he saw you with that other guy . . . frankly, I was scared."

"Even if I believe you, what am I supposed to do?"

"Anything! Anything and everything. Do you want him, yes or no?"

I turned towards the bay window to see if I could catch sight of Edward. He was still on the beach, more lonely and more handsome than ever.

"Of course I do."

"Well then get a move on! Seduce him; shake your booty in front of him; make him realize that *you're* the love of his life, not that bitch. Get your claws out, and the rest. It won't be a clean fight between you and her; no holds barred. You're going to have to be really brave to break through his armor. But you'd better understand that he might drop both of you and disappear someplace where you'd never find him."

9

Judith had just left. She made me swear on the Bible that I would put my plan of attack into action as soon as possible. Except that before marching into battle, I definitely had to recover from my hangover. Just as I was getting ready to go to bed really early, someone knocked on my door. Would this damned day never end? I was so on edge that I nearly burst out laughing when I found the great Megan standing in front of me. No end to it. She looked me up and down and I took advantage to check her out. It was the first time I'd seen her so close up. She was beautiful but cold, haughty, with a proud, hard look in her eyes. Compared to her, any woman would look like a high school kid. She was the very image of the sexy businesswoman away for the weekend, with her expensive jeans, unbelievably spotless high heels, and manicured nails. I might as well admit it, my "morning after the night before" look did not play in my favor.

"Diana, isn't it?"

"No, Diane. What do you want?"

"It seems that Edward rushed to your rescue the other night, didn't he?"

"What business is that of yours?"

"Stop hanging around him. He's mine."

I laughed in her face.

"Laugh if you want, I couldn't care less. Don't waste your time. You're not his type. I mean really, look at yourself."

She had a look of disgust on her face.

"Is that the best you can do?" I asked. "Because if you think I'm going to step aside for you, you've got another think coming."

She smiled at me maliciously.

"So you made him feel sorry for you, is that it?" she asked.

I couldn't catch my breath; my legs started shaking, tears rushed to my eyes; I had to steady myself against the doorframe.

"Poor little thing," Megan added.

I could hear the distant sound of a motor. She snorted.

"Perfect. Here's Edward. He's about to see you at your best."

He got out of the car and immediately walked over to us.

"What are you doing here?" he asked Megan.

I purposely kept my head down.

"I heard Diane's terrible story and came to give her my condolences about her husband and daughter."

She gushed sincerity.

"Are you done?"

His tone of voice was so harsh that I looked up. He was staring daggers at her. But she kept a look of utter solicitude on her face. She turned to me and put a hand on my arm.

"I'm sorry; I didn't mean to open old wounds. If you need us, please don't hesitate. And as soon as you feel better, we can go and have a drink, just us girls. It would do you good . . ."

"That's enough Megan," Edward cut in. "You've made your point. Take the keys and go into the house."

She gave me a peck on the cheek. The kiss of Judas. She turned on her heels but quickly changed her mind.

"Are you coming Edward?"

"No. I need to talk to Diane."

She took it with a smile. My morale suddenly improved. She walked up to him.

"Take your time. I'm going to make us a romantic little supper."

She stood on tiptoe and kissed the corner of his mouth. I saw Edward's hand around her waist. I fell flat again, like a balloon that had just burst. Megan winked at me and headed for Edward's place. I knew I was looking at him all wide-eyed but I couldn't help myself. He brushed his hair back and couldn't look at me. He was obviously wondering why he'd decided to stay. I would make it easier for him.

"Don't keep her waiting."

"What got into you the other night?"

"I had to drown my sorrows."

We looked deep into each other's eyes for a long time.

"What do you expect of me?" he finally asked.

"That you take control of your life, and . . . make certain decisions."

He lit a cigarette and turned away.

"It's complicated. I can't give you an answer, not now."

He started walking away, without saying another word.

"Edward."

He stopped.

"Don't shut me out of your life."

"Even if I wanted to, it would be impossible."

And with that, he walked towards his house. Megan must have been watching us; she came outside when he got to the steps. She pulled him close and dragged him inside. The war had begun, and Megan already had a huge advantage. She knew him inside and out, what to say and when. They had a past together and she could use that as a weapon. As for me, I was always walking on eggshells with him. Apart from a few fights as neighbors that were sometimes more serious than others, and a truce that lasted a few weeks, when all was said and done, what had Edward and I actually done together? I fell asleep thinking about that.

Megan hadn't spent the night at his place, though that didn't really mean anything. She'd just arrived. Edward had been on the beach for quite a while with his camera. I laughed to myself watching Megan trying to walk in the sand in her stilettos. I thought I would wet myself when Postman Pat jumped on her. That weird and wonderful dog was definitely my best friend. He'd been for a swim and had rolled around in the sand just before she got there, and Megan's magnificent cashmere coat was paying the price. Suddenly, it hit me. I knew what I shared with Edward, and Megan couldn't compete with me on my home ground.

My hat and scarf, in pure wool of course, would be my seductive trump cards. Unbelievable. I walked towards the beach, light-hearted and determined to show that stupid woman she hadn't gotten rid of me. She didn't notice me standing right behind her. She was talking to herself: "No way I'm going to rot in this place. I'll get him back to Dublin in a flash, and once and for all. And he'll have that horrible dog put to sleep at the same time."

The bitch!

"Hello Megan!" I said, walking past her.

I whistled. Postman Pat ran over to me. He jumped on me; I stood and petted him. He started jumping and yapping when he saw me pick up a stick. I threw it for him, winked at my rival, and continued walking down the beach. Edward saw me from a distance. I waved at him and continued playing with the dog. He knew I was there, that was enough. Surreptitiously, I walked towards him, but I didn't look at him, I just concentrated on the dog.

"Diane," I heard him call.

It was difficult to hide my smile. I was just about to turn towards him when Postman Pat knocked me over. Of course, I was holding the stick. I rolled around in the sand, shaking with uncontrollable laughter. It was exactly what I'd wanted. And my fellow conspirator joined in when he came over and licked my face. Postman Pat grabbed the stick from me and took off. I opened my eyes. Edward was standing over me, one leg on each side of my body. I noticed his features looked drawn, his eyes had dark circles under them. But he was smiling at me.

"If you only knew what a state you're in!"

"If you only knew how little I care!"

He stretched his hands out to me and I took hold of them; he helped me up. We stood like that for a few moments. Then, he brushed a bit of sand off my face with his thumb. I could see the signs of affection on his face that he'd had for me in the recent past. Now was the time.

"Walk with me a little?" I suggested.

His hand, still resting against my face, dropped down; he glanced towards the sea, then turned to me.

"I was going home; I have pictures to develop."

Recreation time was over. He went to pick up his cameras. I sighed. But I was really surprised when I saw him walking back to me.

"Are you still interested in the photos from the Aran Islands?"

"Of course."

"Come with me and I'll give them to you."

We walked along the beach in silence. For a few moments, I almost forgot Megan was there. She was waiting for us, leaning against her car.

"What are you doing here?" Edward asked her, harshly. "You hate the beach and always have."

"I wanted to see you. I need to talk to you about my plans."

"I have no time now; I've got work to do."

"I can wait."

Edward kept walking and I followed him. Megan followed me. What would you have to say to her to make her understand she was in the way? He opened the door and went inside. I stopped at the doorstep. Megan pushed me aside without him seeing and followed him inside.

"I told you, not now," he said again when he saw her.

"Well, what is *she* doing here?"

"Edward has some photos to give me, that's all. Then I'm going to leave him in peace."

He went upstairs. I lit a cigarette. Megan didn't budge an inch. A real guard dog in high heels. Two minutes later, Edward ran down the stairs holding a large envelope. He handed it to me without a word.

"Thank you," I said. "See you later."

"Whenever you like."

I smiled one last time before heading for the door. I could hear Megan pleading with him to let her stay. But he threw her out.

I was at my front door when she came storming over.

"Wait a minute, you!" I heard Megan say to me.

After all, I did deserve to enjoy my victory that day. I turned around and gave her my most hypocritical smile. Her anger made her look ugly.

"What are those photos?"

"Oh, these?" I asked, waving the envelope in her face.

"Cut it out!"

"They're photos that Edward took of me and the two of us on the Aran Islands."

"You're lying!"

"You don't believe me? Yet, it's absolutely true. And the bed and breakfast was wonderful, such comfortable beds, the ideal spot for two people in love."

"Give me that!"

She grabbed the photos from me. Even though I was a nonbeliever, I prayed to the Good Lord that I hadn't exaggerated. When I saw Megan's face distorted with both rage and jealousy, I promised myself I'd light a candle at the first church I could find. Abby would help me.

"It isn't possible," she said, over and over again.

"But it is."

If her eyes had been machine guns, I would have been riddled with bullets. She threw the photos in my face and walked to her car.

"You'll pay for this!"

I glanced at the first picture. If I'd been her, I would have had a fit. I was completely flustered. I didn't even bother answering her and went inside to study the photos in detail.

The next evening, I decided to go to the pub in the hope of running into Edward. The owner gave me a big smile. I climbed up onto a barstool.

"I'm really sorry about the last time."

"No worries, it happens to everyone," he replied, serving me a pint. "It's on the house."

"Thank you."

He glanced over at the door, raised his eyes to heaven, and turned to me.

"Good luck."

"I'm sorry, what?"

"Hello, Diane," Megan said.

She gracefully hoisted herself up next to me and ordered a glass of white wine. If Edward turned up, I wouldn't look good compared to her. No man could resist her, there was no denying it. She was gorgeous, in a black dress that was neither vulgar nor seductive. It was sexy, classy, showing just enough flesh to make men want to see more.

"I have a proposition for you," she said after a few moments.

I looked at her, even more suspicious than ever.

"I'm prepared to admit that there's something going on between you," she began. "You're a worthy opponent, so I can't help admiring you."

News to me.

"Get to the point."

"Edward belongs to me, no matter what you do, but he's got you on his mind and I have to deal with it. So I propose to disappear for a few days; you can seduce him and sleep together. That way, he can move on . . . and come back to me."

"I think you need to see a doctor."

"Don't play the prude. Something tells me that you haven't had a man in your bed since your husband died."

I wanted to throw up.

"You know, getting back to the joys of sex with Edward is a very good way to ease yourself back in. I'm doing you a favor, actually."

This was becoming really sleazy. I couldn't string two words together.

"You refuse? Too bad."

She glanced at me one last time before getting her phone out of her bag and dialing a number.

"Edward, it's me," she simpered. "I'm at the pub . . . I was thinking about you. Can we see each other tonight? . . . We need to talk . . ."

As the conversation continued, her voice changed, becoming softer, more tender. She fiddled with an imaginary crumb in her hand.

"I'm really sorry about yesterday. I know you need to be alone to work."

I couldn't hear Edward's replies, but I could guess by what Megan was saying.

"And I shouldn't have reproached you for spending time with Diane," she continued. "You're a good man, you're helping her get back on her feet. It really wasn't my place after what I did to you."

I was going crazy. Edward couldn't possibly be that gullible!

"But it's so hard to see you with another woman," she whimpered. "I know how badly I hurt you. I want to go back to the way things were between us . . . like before . . ."

It was laughable. It couldn't work. Impossible. Edward wouldn't fall into such an obvious trap. He wouldn't let himself get back into the claws of this tigress who tried to pass herself off as a harmless little kitten.

"I'm begging you," she whispered. "Say yes. Just for tonight, please. We can talk about me moving here . . ."

An evil smile spread across her face.

"Thank you . . ." she sighed, sounding as if she were about to die. "I'll wait for you."

What a moron! The bitch hung up, got a mirror from her bag, and checked her makeup. She put it away and turned to me.

"Edward will never change. I know exactly what he wants to hear."

"You're disgusting. How can you talk about him like that? And all your lies?"

She swept away my remark with the back of her hand.

"A bit of advice: don't spend your whole evening waiting for him."

She burst out laughing.

"Poor Diane. I warned you!"

I headed out to the terrace. I took long drags on my cigarette like a fanatic.

When I went back inside the pub, I found that Edward had arrived. He and Megan were getting ready to leave. She put her arm around his waist and he let her. I clenched my fists. She was the first to notice me.

"Isn't that Diane over there?" she asked him.

"Yes," he replied, looking at me.

She dragged him over to me. Edward and I stared into each other's eyes.

"Hello," Megan said. "What a shame, I didn't know you were here; we could have had a drink together and really gotten to know each other."

She smiled at me looking extremely kind. Edward was watching her with an expression I hadn't seen on him before. Dumbfounded by the talent of Megan the actress, I let her keep talking without managing to put her in her place.

"We'll have to say goodbye, I reserved a table. We'll get together soon, all right?"

Completely thrown, I nodded like an idiot.

"Go wait for me in the car," Edward told her.

She gave him a peck on the cheek then said "See you soon" to me. I watched her go. So did Edward. She stopped at the door, turned around and gave us a wave.

"Are you really going to spend the evening with her?"

"We need to talk."

"Don't forget what she did to you."

Edward's expression hardened.

"You don't know her."

"Don't let her hurt you."

"She's changed."

He turned and was about to leave, but I held him back by his coat.

"Are you really sure about that?"

"Good night."

I let go of him; he looked at me one last time, turned, and left.

He didn't get home until late that night. I knew he'd locked himself in his darkroom when I saw the red light filtering through the blinds. Megan must have failed.

My hopes were dashed the next morning when I saw the two of them on the beach. I watched them, hidden behind my bedroom curtains. She wouldn't let go of him, smiling and batting her eyelashes, I was sure of it. Yet, he was keeping her at a distance. They headed up to the cottages and he walked her to her car. They stood facing each other. I could make out Edward's blank expression; she put her hands on his chest. He shook his head and pulled away. Megan stood on tiptoe to kiss him on the cheek. She got into her car and left. He lit a cigarette before shutting himself away in his house.

A few hours later, someone knocked on my door. I opened it and found Edward there.

"Can I come in?"

I stood aside and he went into the living room. He seemed nervous, walking in circles.

"Do you have something you want to tell me?"

"I'm leaving."

"What do you mean, you're leaving?"

He turned around and walked over to me.

"I'm only going away for a few days. I need some space."

"I understand. What about Megan? What is she doing?"

"She's staying at the hotel."

I stroked his cheek; it was full of stubble. Then I ran a finger over the dark circles under his eyes. He was looking more and more exhausted. He couldn't stand any more.

"Take care of yourself."

He kept staring at me. To my great surprise, he

took me in his arms, held me close, and buried his head in my neck. I held onto him and couldn't hold back the tears. He looked up, kissed me on the forehead, let go of me, and left without a word.

As soon as he was gone, I felt miserable. I wandered around my cottage like a lost soul.

The days passed and each one seemed the same. The tension dissipated. I didn't go out. I didn't want to run into Megan and start playing her childish games again. No surprise that Edward had run away. I didn't hear from him, but that didn't surprise me. I spent hours sitting in an armchair, opposite Mulranny Bay. I thought back to the time when Colin and Clara had died, my coming to Ireland, meeting Edward.

One afternoon, my phone rang. Felix. I hesitated a few seconds before answering.

"Hi."

"Still sober?"

"You can be so silly sometimes. What's new in Paris?"

"Oh, nothing special. What about you?"

"Me neither."

"You sound peculiar. Are you OK?"

"Yes, yes, everything's fine."

"What are you doing?"

"I'm thinking about my future."

"And?"

"I have no idea, but I hope to find some answers soon."

"Keep me posted."

"I promise. OK, I'll say goodbye now."

I hung up and lit a cigarette.

Edward had been gone a week. A week when I'd gone over the situation from every angle, imagining every possible outcome. When someone knocked on my door late that afternoon, I knew it was the moment of truth.

Edward stood at the door, looking serious. He looked deep into my eyes and I was afraid. My heart was racing. Without saying a word, he came inside and stood in front of the bay window. I followed him and stood a few feet away. He passed one hand over his face and sighed deeply.

"When Megan showed up, I was overwhelmed by what was happening. I was afraid of what was going to happen. Though I already knew the answer, and I'd known for a long time. If I'd been honest with myself from the beginning, I could have avoided this whole mess."

"What are you trying to tell me?" I asked, my voice shaking.

"I asked Megan to leave, to go back to Dublin."

"Are you sure?"

"She's out of my life, once and for all. It's over. Now, it's just the two of us, just you and me."

I couldn't speak. I looked at him; never before had he been so calm, so relaxed. He smiled at me, came over, and held me by the waist. I clutched onto his shirt so I wouldn't fall. I couldn't look at him, his expression was so intense. He leaned his forehead against mine.

"Diane . . . I want a real relationship with you . . . You're the one I . . ."

I put one finger over his lips. Silence filled the room; it was so quiet I could hear my heart beating. I saw my hands against his chest; I could feel his breath against my skin. I gently pulled away. I walked over to the couch and collapsed onto it. He followed me, sat on the coffee table opposite me, and took my hands in his.

"We'll start over, from the beginning," he said. "Don't worry."

I looked into his eyes. The tenderness and love I saw in them was overwhelming. I couldn't wait any longer; I had to say something.

"Listen to me, all right?"

He smiled at me; I squeezed his hands. I breathed in deeply before starting to speak.

"I didn't think it would be so hard . . . while you were away, I thought a lot about everything that happened to us since I got here. You came into my life and I wanted to fight, to laugh, to live again . . . You became so important to me, almost essential . . . I believed in that . . . I believed so much, but . . . in fact, I was deluding myself by hoping you would fill the void within me and . . . that . . . I could love again . . ."

I was overcome with emotion. I made no effort to hold back the tears. My hands were shaking; I squeezed his tighter. I could tell from his expression how much I was hurting him. But I had to finish what I'd started.

"But I'm not ready . . . I'm too haunted by the past. I can't shut out Colin the way you just did with Megan. If I start a relationship with you, I'll resent you some day for not being him . . . for being you. And I don't want that . . . you aren't my crutch or some cure; you deserve to be loved unconditionally, for you alone, not for your healing powers. And I know . . . that I don't love you the way I should. Not yet, anyway. First I have to get back to being myself, become strong again, feel good on my own, without anyone's help. Then, and only then, I'll be able to love again. Completely. Do you understand?"

He dropped my hands as if I were burning him. He clenched his teeth. I got my breath back, stared into space before delivering the final blow:

"I'm leaving, because I can't be near you."

Or far from you, I thought. My tears kept falling; we looked at each other.

"I have my plane ticket. In a few days, I'll be leaving Mulranny; I'm going back to Paris. I have to finish building my life, and I have to do it alone, without you."

I tried to take his hand. He pulled away.

"Forgive me," I whispered.

He closed his eyes, clenched his fists, and took a deep breath. Then, without looking at me, he got up and headed for the door.

"Wait," I begged, running after him.

He opened the door halfway, left it open, ran to his car, got in, and left. At that moment, I realized I'd never see him again. And it hurt. It hurt very much.

The easiest part of all was telling Felix. I called him.

"You again!" he said when he'd picked up.

"Yep . . . are you ready to put up with me again?"

"What?"

"I'm coming home."

"You're doing what?"

"I'm coming back to Paris."

"*Hooray!* I'll plan a big party. And you'll move in with me . . ."

"Stop. Absolutely no party. And I'm going to live in the studio above Happy People."

"You're crazy; it's a hovel."

"It's just fine. And it means we'll be able to open on time."

"Because you're planning to come back to work? Tell me another."

"And yet, it's true. See you at Happy People."

"Not so fast, I'll pick you up at the airport."

"Not necessary. I'll manage by myself. I know how to do that now."

Three hours later, with a heavy heart, I went to see Abby and Jack. Judith opened the door.

"What are you doing here?" I asked.

She threw her arms around my neck.

"Where's my brother? I ran into the slut last night; she was trying to pick up anyone she could in a pub. I jumped into my car to come and congratulate you."

"I'm glad you're here. I need to talk to all three of you."

"What's going on?"

"Let's go see Abby and Jack."

She let me pass. Abby gave me a hug and kept calling me "darling". Judith must have given them a heads-up. She must have told them that Edward and I were deeply in love. My eyes misted up. I noticed Jack's knowing look; he'd already understood. I was about to kill the atmosphere.

We sat down. Abby and Judith were fidgeting on the couch. Only Jack kept his cool; he was watching me.

"You're leaving, aren't you?" he asked.

"Yes."

"What? What are you talking about?" Judith cried.

"My life is in Paris."

"What about Edward?"

I lowered my head and my whole body drooped.

"I thought you loved him. You're no better than her; you took advantage of him and now you're dropping him!"

"Judith, that's enough," Abby cut in.

"When are you going?"

"The day after tomorrow."

"So soon!" Abby exclaimed.

"It's better that way. There's something else . . . when I explained my decision to Edward, he left and hasn't come home. That was three days ago. I don't know where he is . . . I'm really sorry."

"It's not your fault," Jack said.

Judith leaped off the couch and got out her phone.

"It's his voicemail!" she shouted. "He's going to treat us to his wild animal routine again. We've already been through that once! Now a second time? Fuck!"

Crimson with anger, she threw her phone down and acted like I wasn't there.

"I think I should go," I told them.

I headed for the front door. All three of them followed me. Out of the corner of my eye, I saw Jack put his arms around his wife's shoulders. Sadness and concern were visible on their faces. At the doorstep, Abby gave me a hug.

"Keep in touch."

"Thank you for everything," I replied, fighting back the tears.

I hugged her back, kissed Jack on the cheek, and turned to Judith.

"I'll walk you to your car," she said, without looking at me.

I opened the car door and threw my bag inside. Judith said nothing.

"Have I lost a friend?" I asked.

"You decided to be an idiot! I've already got enough problems managing my brother . . ."

"You'll look out for him?'

"You can trust me to give him a kick up the butt."

"I don't know what to say. I would have wanted it to . . ."

"I know," she cut in, looking me straight in the eyes. "Can I come and see you in Paris if I feel like it?"

"Whenever you like."

I started to cry and saw that Judith's eyes were also filling with tears.

"Get going now."

I hugged her tight before getting in the car. I left without looking back.

I did a big spring clean to erase any trace of my stay. My suitcases were piled up in front of the entrance, then in my car. As I closed the trunk, I looked at the cottage next door, hopelessly empty, no sign of life. My final hours in Ireland passed in great loneliness.

I spent my last night sitting on the couch, waiting for something, no idea what. Dawn had only just broken when I ended my ordeal. I drank some coffee and smoked a cigarette while going around the house.

It was gloomy outside, raining, and strong gusts of wind hit me. Right until the end, I'd have to cope with the Irish weather; I'd miss it.

I felt sick as I locked the door. I leaned my forehead against it. It was time to go; I turned towards my car and froze. Edward was standing there, his face inscrutable. I ran and threw myself into his arms, crying. He held me tight and stroked my hair. I breathed deeply to remember his scent. He kissed me on the forehead, pressing his lips hard against my skin. That gave me the courage to look at him. He put his hand on my cheek and I rested my face against it. I tried to smile but couldn't. I was still clutching him. I let go. He looked deep into my eyes, for the last time, I knew that, and headed for the beach. I got into my car and drove away. My knuckles were white from holding the steering wheel so tight. One last look in the mirror. He was standing there, in the rain, looking at the sea. Tears blurred my vision; I wiped them away with the back of my hand and drove faster.

10

I got out of the taxi in front of Happy People. The driver put my suitcases on the sidewalk. It was closed. No sign of Felix. I stood at the door and pressed my face against the window. Everything was dark and looked dusty. I sat down on one of my suitcases. I lit a cigarette and started looking around.

Back to square one. Nothing had changed: people in a hurry, the awful traffic, the hustle and bustle of the shops. I'd forgotten how miserable Parisians always looked. A training course in Irish human warmth should be required in school. That was what I was thinking, yet I knew full well that in less than two days, I'd have the same pale face and unfriendly expression as them.

I'd been hanging around for an hour. I could see Felix coming towards me, and I thought how much he'd changed. He walked close to the buildings, wearing a hat, hiding behind his jacket collar. When he was standing in front of me, I saw he had an enormous bandage across his face.

"Don't say a word," he said.

I burst out laughing.

"Now I understand why it's closed."

"The only thing that got me out of the house was you coming back."

"Damn, you're really here." (He pinched my cheeks.) "It's crazy, it's like you never left!"

"I feel very strange, you know."

I wrapped his arms around me and started to cry.

"Don't get yourself in such a state over me. It's just a broken nose."

"Idiot."

He crushed me against him and rocked me. I laughed through my tears.

"I can't breathe."

"Do you really want to live up there?"

"Yes; it will be perfect."

"If you want to pretend you're a penniless student, that's your problem."

He helped me carry some of my suitcases. He used his shoulder to push open the door to the building.

"Oh, that really hurts."

I burst out laughing.

"Shut it!"

He handed me the key when we got to the apartment. I opened the door, went inside and was surprised to find a stack of cardboard boxes.

"What's all this?"

"It's what I managed to save when they moved everything out of your apartment. Your parents are real piranhas. I stored everything here until you came back."

"Thank you."

I couldn't stop yawning and Felix couldn't stop talking. He ordered a pizza, for a change, and we shared it, sitting around a crate we used as a coffee table. He told me in detail how he'd broken his nose, a dismal tale that happened after a drunken night out.

"Listen," I cut in, "we have all the time in the world, but now, I'm exhausted, and we have to be in good shape for tomorrow."

"Why?"

"Happy People, mean anything to you?"

"You're not joking; you really want to get back to work?'

All I did was give him a look.

"OK, I got it."

He stood up. I walked him to the door.

"See you tomorrow morning to go over everything," I said.

He felt in his pocket and handed me a bunch of keys.

"In case I don't wake up," he said, kissing me.

"Good night."

He looked at me oddly.

"What?"

"Nothing, we'll talk about it later."

Ten minutes later, I was in bed, but I couldn't fall asleep. I'd forgotten how noisy the city was—car horns, sirens, the night owls, lights always on. Mulranny was very far away. And so was Edward.

I went down the hallway to get into the bookstore. The door creaked. It smelled musty. I switched on the lights. Several bulbs needed changing.

Happy People didn't look good at all. I walked into the room. I thought far back in my memories for the impressions I'd had in the past. Hardly anything was still there. I walked in between the bookshelves; some of them were empty. I ran my hand along the books that were there. I picked one up at random; it was dog-eared and yellowing; the next ones weren't in much better shape. I went behind the counter. I ran my hand along the bar; it was sticky. I glanced at the dishes; the glasses and cups were chipped. A sheet of paper was taped over one of the beer pumps; it was broken. The accounting books and orders were in a mess on the floor. Only the board with photos on it was clean and in the right place. The coffee machine resisted for a long time before finally spitting out a liquid that vaguely looked like coffee. I leaned against the wall and made a face when I tasted it. Moral of the story: never entrust anything to Felix. To hold my own, to stand on my own two feet, to get better, I was going to revive Happy People.

I was mopping the floor for the third time when my dear colleague deigned to show up.

"Are you reinventing yourself as a cleaner?"

"Yes. And so are you."

I threw a pair of rubber gloves in his face.

After cleaning for hours, we sat down on the floor. Dozens of garbage bags were piled high on the sidewalk. Unlike us, Happy People smelled fresh and clean.

"Felix, from now on, you're going to stop pretending to be a librarian."

"So I can pretend to be a salesman?"

I shook my head.

"And you'd better warn your buddies that they're going to have to pay for every last drop they drink, even if it's a glass of water. Understand?"

"You scare me when you're like this."

He raised his arms to protect his face. I gave him a little slap and stood up.

"Go out and play now."

"What are we doing tomorrow?"

"We'll place orders."

"Do you need me?"

"Do grow up. Don't worry, sleeping late in the morning is part of the plan."

Felix and I were each on one side of the bar. I went through all the accounts with a fine-tooth comb while he prepared the orders.

Night had fallen a long time ago.

"Stop! I've had it up to here," he declared.

He stood up, poured us each a glass of wine, and straightened out the accounting books before sitting down on the bar.

"Madam Commander in Chief isn't going to tell me off?"

"No, I was about to announce we had finished for today."

He laughed, clinked glasses with me, and got his pack of cigarettes from under the counter. I gave him my darkest look.

"Please, we're closed; I have the right to have a ciggy. And you won't resist for long."

He waved the cigarette under my nose.

"Fine; give me a ciggy."

I lit it, took a sip of wine, and looked at him.

"Have I changed?"

"Even when Colin and Clara were still here, I never saw you so driven, and what's really crazy is that you can manage all by yourself."

"I think that rebuilding my life has to start here at Happy People. We're lucky to have this place, aren't we?"

"You're not planning on becoming a workaholic, are you? Because if you are, then I resign."

"Given how little you do, that wouldn't be a great loss."

"Seriously, how are you?"

"I'm good."

"Yeees . . . So you'll go out on a binge with me tonight?"

"I don't feel like it."

"You're not going to lock yourself away in your little café forever."

"Some day, I promise, I'll go out and have fun with you."

"You need to see people, and also, I don't know . . . maybe it's time to . . . to meet a nice guy."

I knew that I'd have to tell him everything at some point.

"I think I met him too soon."

Felix sighed.

"Colin has been gone for two years."

"I know."

"You're hopeless; you'll end up an old maid, with cats."

He shook his head and jumped down from the counter.

"I'm going for a pee."

"Good for you," I replied, lighting a cigarette.

Five, four, three, two, one . . .

"Did you meet someone?" he shouted when he came out of the bathroom.

"Your fly's open . . ."

"Answer me! Who is it? Where is he? Do I know him?"

"Yes."

"Edward! You got it on with the Irishman. I was sure of it. Well? I want all the juicy details!"

"There's nothing to tell. I'll sum up the situation very simply for you. He was very good for me, I hurt him a lot, and I've surely lost him forever. And that's all there is to tell."

"You couldn't hurt a fly, so a guy like that, impossible."

He came and put his arms around me and crushed me to him, as he always did.

"Come on . . . tell me what happened."

"Please, I don't want to talk about him."

"Why?"

"Because I miss him."

I curled up even closer in his arms.

"Thank goodness you didn't bring him back in your suitcase. That would have been really bad. I would have constantly wanted to jump on your guy."

I cried. From laughing. And from sadness. Felix rocked me in his arms for a long time before I managed to calm down.

Happy People was ready. Me, not so much. I'd hardly slept and was both anxious and excited at the same time. I inspected the place one last time. Everything was sparkling clean: the new dishes were all in place, the beer pump was in perfect working order, the coffee machine produced a brew worthy of the name, the counter was shiny, and the brand new books were nicely arranged and displayed, waiting on their shelves for their readers.

Felix and I had decided to dust off our catalogue, in every way. I'd given him carte blanche because it had been too long since I'd taken any interest in what was happening in the literary world to be up to date. "We have to have some really modern, fun things," he'd said. "We have customers who like that, you know." I had no doubt, especially since he was the one who brought those customers in. So he had ordered, among others, some Chuck Palahniuk, Irvine Welsh, and the latest novel of a French author I didn't know, Laurent Bettoni.

The book was called *Earthly Bodies*. "You'll see, it's as if Sade had written *Dangerous Liaisons* but in a very modern style," Felix told me. "It will bring us a little whiff of scandal that will be really nice." I'd smiled. After two years of lethargy, I felt eager for some lust and scandal.

Here we go: the "Open" sign hung on the door. I opened it to listen to the little bell, like in the past, when it made Clara so happy. I closed my eyes and saw her smile. The first customer came in. The day had begun.

Felix arrived around noon carrying an enormous bouquet of roses and freesias, just like the one Colin had brought me all those years before. He handed it to me, somewhat embarrassed, and went to hang his jacket in the coat closet. I found somewhere to put the flowers and went over to him. I stood on tiptoe and gave him a kiss on the cheek.

"He'd be proud of you," he whispered in my ear.

I spent Sunday getting my apartment in order. I'd been back for two weeks and was still living in the middle of boxes and suitcases. It wasn't a very big place, but it was just what I needed. I felt safe there and at home. I hung a few pictures of Colin and Clara on the walls, so they'd be with me. My clothes, and only mine, were hung in the closet. I put the books I'd taken to Ireland in the bookcase. And it gave me great pleasure to take out the coffee pot Colin had bought for me. I owed Felix a great deal for having saved it.

Only one suitcase left to empty. I found Edward's photos inside. Unable to resist, I sat down on the floor to look at them. When I saw the two of us on the glossy paper, I was overcome with memories and doubts once more. I thought about Edward constantly. I was worried about him. I wanted to know how he was, what he was doing, what he'd say if he knew I'd gone back to work. I wanted to know if he was thinking about me. I put the photos away in a box filled with other memories, right at the back of a closet. I sighed, turned on some music, and headed for the bathroom. I let the water flow over my body while thinking that the next day, I'd wake up to start a new week at work. I'd manage to get up at seven thirty, I'd get out of bed, dress, and open the bookstore. I'd find the strength to smile at the customers and talk to them. I'd make it work; I had no choice.

*

The sun shone through the curtains in my bedroom, which was going to help me accomplish my goal for the day. I'd been here a month and didn't want to go backwards. I took my time getting ready. I opened the window and sat in front of it to drink my coffee and smoke my first cigarette.

Like every morning, I went into the bookstore through the back door. But today, I put a sign in the window to announce we'd be opening late. I was running on automatic pilot.

I went to the florist and came out carrying an armful of white roses. Flushed, I wandered along the paths. Though I knew the way.

I took a deep breath and stood up tall once I got to their grave. It was as well cared for as ever. I pulled a few dying petals off of the tombstone and arranged my flowers in a vase. I crouched down to their level. I ran my fingers over their names.

"Hi! I've come back . . . my darlings . . . I missed you . . . Ireland was good, but it would have been better with you both there. Clara, my love, if you only knew . . . I rolled around in the sand with a big dog, bigger than you'd ever seen; you could have climbed on his back and given him lots of hugs . . . I'm sorry you didn't have a dog like him . . . Mama loves you . . ."

I wiped a tear that rolled down my cheek.

"Colin . . . my love . . . I love you too much. When will I finally be ready to let you go? I was very close, but then, you saw what happened . . . I think you'd like Edward . . . What am I saying? I'm the one who has to like him, aren't I?"

I looked around, seeing nothing. I wiped away my tears. Then I looked at their gravestone again and leaned my head to one side.

"I love you both so much . . . But I have to go; Felix is waiting for me."

I'd just arrived in front of my literary café. Felix wasn't there, naturally. But the sky was still blue. I smiled and closed my eyes. I was capable of enjoying life's simple pleasures. That was already an accomplishment; that was already better. I touched my wedding ring. One day, I would take it off. For Edward, perhaps. I heard the telephone ringing. Time to get to work. Before going inside, I glanced at the sign.

Happy People . . .

Acknowledgments

My thanks to:

Laurent Bettoni, author, educator, and trail blazer. Thank you for having believed more than I did, for pushing me to my limits, with your wisdom and without concessions. Thanks to you, I know what kind of author I want to be.

My first readers, from the beginning. You were the starting point of the adventure called *Happy People* . . . since December 2012.

To Éditions Michel Lafon and Florian Lafani. Thanks for having gone off the beaten track and respecting my journey and my freedom.